Tangled Heritage

*Also by Jane Edwards
in Large Print:*

Yellow Ribbons
Dangerous Odyssey
The Hesitant Heart
The Ghost of Castle Kilgarrom
Susannah is Missing!

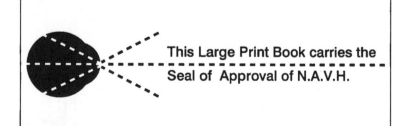

Tangled Heritage

Jane Edwards

Thorndike Press • Thorndike, Maine

Published in 1999 by arrangement with Jane Edwards.

Thorndike Large Print® Candlelight Series.

The tree indicium is a trademark of Thorndike Press.

The text of this Large Print edition is unabridged.
Other aspects of the book may vary from the original edition.

Set in 16 pt. Plantin.

Printed in the United States on permanent paper.

Library of Congress Cataloging in Publication Data

Edwards, Jane (Jane Campbell), 1932–
    Tangled heritage / Jane Edwards.
        p.   cm.
    ISBN 0-7862-1739-1 (lg. print : hc : alk. paper)
    1. Large type books.   I. Title.
    [PS3555.D933T36   1999]
    813'.54—dc21   98-48516

With love to my favorite cousin,
Mary Virginia Kampmeier
of Graceville, Minnesota,
who shares the Campbell
half of my heritage.

I am indebted to
the Humboldt County
Chamber of Commerce,
Eureka, California,
and to the staff of the Ferndale Museum
for research assistance,
and to Ken and Norma Bessingpas,
owners of The Shaw House,
for their warm and wonderful hospitality.
Thank you all.

Chapter One

"You inherited a *what?*"

Lindsay Dorsett could hardly blame her friend for sounding incredulous. She herself was still trying to come to terms with the unexpected legacy.

Clutching a section of the old-fashioned telephone in each hand, she leaned back against the apple-green plush of the curly-legged chair. "A 'Butterfat' mansion," she repeated. "It's a stately Queen Anne Victorian, with bay windows and a turret and twelve-foot-high ceilings."

"And gingerbready carvings above all the doors and windows? Ugh!" Ceci Havershaw's aversion to such an obsolete style of architecture all but shuddered across the 260 miles of telephone line separating the two young women. "It sounds downright prehistoric!"

"Well, historic, anyway." Lindsay tamped down a flicker of annoyance. "In fact, the entire town has been designated a state historical landmark."

She explained that Ferndale was located

on California's scenic north coast, a few miles south of Eureka. Long before the turn of the century it had become known as the Cream City.

"It lies four or five miles inland from the sea, in the heart of a lush, wide valley," she elaborated. "Many of the earliest settlers were dairymen who emigrated from places like Denmark and the Swiss Alps."

"I'm picturing Heidi and Grandfather."

"Seems to me they raised goats, but you've got the general idea," Lindsay conceded. "Anyhow, Ferndale kept most of northern California supplied with butter for decades. The owners of those prolific herds used the profits to build themselves sumptuous three- and four-story homes."

"So that's where the name came from!"

Lindsay laughed. "Inevitable, wouldn't you say? Their descendants have been living in these wonderful old Butterfat mansions ever since. You should see the place, Ceci. It's a darling little town. Like a picture postcard of Brigadoon, or someplace that's been completely bypassed by the twentieth century."

"I happen to like the twentieth century," her roommate retorted. "As far as I'm concerned, the past was full of dust catchers. How did you get involved with an anti-

8

quated place like that, anyway? I thought your ancestors were from New Hampshire."

"They are — on Dad's side of the family. There's been a Dorsett in the diplomatic corps since the days of Benjamin Franklin," Lindsay said proudly. "But my mother's people came from Portugal. They were seafarers, like Magellan and Dias and Vasco da Gama. My great-grandfather, Bartolomew da Silva, was captaining a fast, oceangoing schooner before he was out of his teens. In the 1890s he and his bride emigrated from the old country and settled in California. Bartolomew went into business transporting cargo up and down the Pacific Coast and made a fortune."

"I suppose it was inevitable he'd want one of those ornate Butterfat mansions for his own family," Ceci said with distaste. "So now the ugly monstrosity has come down to you?"

Lindsay wanted to snap that the house *wasn't* an ugly monstrosity. Just old and rather shabby. But she kept the argument to herself. To Ceci, those terms were bound to mean the same thing.

She stuck to facts. "I'm the last of the line. Apparently the da Silva men had an awful habit of going off and getting killed

9

in wars. On top of that, several of the women, like Great-Aunt Felice, never got married at all."

"She's the one who left you the house?"

"Uh-huh. I met her once, when I was six," Lindsay confided. "That was twenty years ago, and she must have been at least seventy then. My mother died a few years later. What with bouncing all over the globe with Dad on his assignments for the State Department, we never did make a second visit to Ferndale. By the time I finished college and came to live in San Francisco, I had practically forgotten about my da Silva relatives. It never occurred to me that Felice might still be alive."

"Nobody could blame you for not staying in touch."

"I know. Even so, I wish things had been different."

Lindsay gazed around the generously proportioned parlor. It was nearly as large as the whole high-rise apartment shared by Ceci and herself and their friend Anita. And this was only one of several living rooms, salons, drawing rooms — "offices," she thought they had once been called on the ground floor of the house. The formerly rich crimsons, golds, and greens of the Aubusson rug had faded, while the wallpaper had mellowed to a muted shade of rose. But above the arching marble mantel the pair of portraits in heavy gold frames still appeared vibrantly alive, even though the paintings must have been completed nearly ninety years earlier.

Family portraits, Lindsay mused. *Her* family. What had they been like, the people who had lived here so long ago?

An impatient sound from Ceci reminded her that her friend was still on the line. Lindsay dragged her attention back to the phone.

"Now I have a tough decision to make," she said. "The house, along with everything in it, is mine. Luckily the taxes are paid up for the rest of the year. But there's no money left for upkeep or repairs, and I have an awful feeling that a house this size requires plenty of both. I don't know how I'm going to handle the problem."

"What's to handle? First thing tomorrow get in touch with a real estate agent. You *are* allowed to sell the place, aren't you?"

"Yes, with one exception." Lindsay recalled a peculiar stipulation in her aunt's will. "The da Silvas apparently had a long-standing feud with a local family named Thorvaldsen. I'm not allowed to sell the mansion to any member of that clan. If I tried, Felice's estate would go to charity instead of to me."

"Then specify that fact in writing when you sign the contract with the realtor and list the old place for sale before you head on back to the city," Ceci advised. "California's real estate market is booming again. Watch and see, someone will offer you a bundle to take that white elephant off your hands. They'll have it transformed into a bed-and-breakfast inn by the middle of the summer."

Several of Ferndale's most elegant Butterfat mansions had already been converted into lodgings open to the public, Lindsay acknowledged. They seemed to do a flourishing business too. But even if she knew anything about running an inn, she lacked the bankroll to tackle any expensive renovations herself. More bathrooms, new wiring, an updated kitchen, and only the building inspector knew what all else would be needed to bring the hundred-year-old house up to the standards offered by the Shaw House or the Gingerbread Mansion.

Yet the notion of handing the property over to some stranger was hateful. She had fallen in love with the house before she was halfway up the front walk. The instant she stepped inside, she had a feeling of home-coming. As for casually discarding the heritage she had just rediscovered —

"No!"

Lindsay flushed with embarrassment at the vehemence with which the word had exploded from her lips. "Sorry, Ceci," she apologized. "I'll probably end up taking your advice. But decisions that irreversible shouldn't be made on the spur of the moment. I've decided to stick around for a while and think things over."

"What about your job?"

"Before leaving the city I arranged to take a couple of weeks' vacation," Lindsay said. "I'm long overdue for a break. The last few years I've put in so much overtime that I sometimes wonder whether there's life after work."

"You should complain, with a soaring career like yours? Name me another woman your age who's responsible for two trendy fashion boutiques in the city's best locations. Incidentally," Ceci added, "I spotted an item about your company in this morning's *Chronicle*. The business analyst predicted that Denim Ala Mode is on the verge of embarking on a major expansion program. You could be in line for a promotion."

"I'm not sure I want it," Lindsay confessed. "Lately I've talked to a number of women who are starting to crumble from the strain of living on the fast track twenty-four hours a day. Is success really worth that sort of stress?"

"Anyone who prefers failure needs their head examined. You'll come to your senses after vegetating up there at the back of beyond for a few days," Ceci predicted. "You'd die of boredom if you sat around any longer than that."

"I didn't plan on sitting around," Lindsay assured her. "It will be a major job just finding out what all this house contains. So far I've lost my way twice while wandering around the ground floor. There are eight or ten bedrooms upstairs, with an acre of attic on top of them that I haven't so much as taken a peek at yet."

"Just don't stay away too long," Ceci warned. "A colleague of Anita's was over last night, raving about our apartment. She kept emphasizing how close it was to everything."

"Well," Lindsay said, only half joking, "if I'm not back by the end of the month, you can rent her my room."

After hanging up, she sat where she was for a few minutes longer, letting the peace and quiet of the old house flow over her. Just staring around at the century-old accumulation of possessions was fascinating. The belongings cherished by three generations of her ancestors represented a tangible sign of continuity.

The things they had lived with told her a lot about her mother's family. They also whetted her appetite to know more.

Lindsay found this sudden need surprising. Always before, she had been so intent on her future that she seldom spared a thought for the past. Now a strange awareness of her origins had come elbowing its way into her consciousness.

Almost from birth she had been a world traveler. Her father had been posted to Istanbul when she was only a few months old. After that, Peter Dorsett had served in the American Embassy in Montevideo, Uruguay. They had just returned from Thailand, she remembered, the time she and her parents had come here to visit Great-Aunt Felice. Very early in life she had been taught the value of her American citizenship. But until today she had never really considered the roots that anchored it. Now she saw herself as a link in a chain. A long, long chain of men and women whose bloodlines she shared.

It felt sad to be the last link.

Lindsay raised solemn brown eyes to the portraits occupying the place of honor above the marble fireplace. Bartolomew and Luzia da Silva would have been around the age she was now when those paintings were commissioned. She ignored the out-of-date hairstyles and obsolete fashions that always made people of earlier generations look so different from their modern-day counterparts and strained to think of her great-grandparents as real people. Courageous people, she felt sure, seeing the determination in their firm mouths and stubborn chins. It would have taken plenty of gumption to leave the land of their birth and set out on the incredibly long, dangerous voyage from Portugal to California. But here in this pleasant valley lying between the wide blue Pacific and towering groves of redwood trees, they had sunk down their roots and flourished.

According to the banker who'd passed on the key to the mansion, the first generation of da Silvas to come to the New World had both triumphs and tragedies to face. Bartolomew's shipping business had made him rich, and six children were born to the couple. Their eldest daughter had died in the terrible worldwide influenza epidemic that killed more than twenty million people in 1918–1919. Prior to that, their two elder sons had gone to fight in the Great War and never returned.

Their fourth and fifth children were both girls. Less than a year separated Felice and Renae in age. Ten years behind his sisters came Manoel, the baby of the family and Lindsay's grandfather. Today she had learned that he died in World War II when his only child, Mercedes — her mother — was tiny.

Now there was nobody left but her.

"I'm sorry," she whispered to those still, solemn faces high up on the wall. "Truly sorry that I can't continue the da Silva name for you. It's bad enough that your boys all died in wars. But why, I wonder, didn't your daughters marry and give you lots and lots of grandchildren?"

Even a cursory examination of Luzia's portrait was enough to show Lindsay where her own cloud of raven's-wing hair had come from. Her mother had inherited that glossy black crowning glory too, along with thick, high-arched brows above luminous brown eyes. Bartolomew's firm chin, marked by a shallow cleft, had come down to them both, as well. Given the family genes, Lindsay suspected that Felice and

Renae had been strikingly attractive women. And the da Silvas had been a long way from poor. They'd had it all — except husbands and children of their own.

But that really wasn't her main concern. Whatever had kept the daughters of Bartolomew and Luzia single, the fact remained that Lindsay herself was the only one left with da Silva blood in her veins. She'd been left an impressive inheritance. Now she had the responsibility of deciding how to handle it.

Throwing open a set of French doors, she stepped out onto a side patio. The flower-scented, mid-April afternoon was a thing of beauty. But although the banker had mentioned hiring someone to cut the grass and prune some of the foliage, the yard still had a rather unkempt look to it.

"Careful that you don't disappear into that jungle of wisteria, or tumble headfirst into Francis Creek," he'd warned. "The last few years this big place got to be too much for old Miss Felice to handle. The fish pond needs to be drained and cleaned, and in my opinion the gazebo should have been torn down years ago."

Catching a glimpse of the old-fashioned summerhouse through branches laden with apple blossoms, Lindsay realized that he had not exaggerated in calling the creek-side structure a derelict. Open to the elements except for four posts holding up its domed roof, the circular gazebo resembled an ancient carousel marooned in a park where children no longer played.

Before she could explore further, an echoing noise, rhythmically repeated, claimed her attention. She turned her head and caught her breath as she focused on the side fence separating her yard from the grounds of its next-door neighbor.

The hammering continued without pause as Lindsay changed direction. The five-foot-high fence had been built on top of a retaining wall. Drawing near to look through the boards, she realized that the adjacent garden lay on a lower plot of ground. Because of the steep drop, even a tall adult standing on the grass down there would need to crane his neck to look up at her.

With painful sharpness, memory flooded over her. That was exactly what had happened the one other time she had stood on this side, peering down into the next yard.

Back then, of course, she had been much shorter. The fence had seemed very tall to her. Far too high to look over, certainly. Yet Lindsay Dorsett had never backed away from a challenge in all her six years. Today it was the sound of hammering that had lured her over. On that long-ago occasion it was the shrill, happy voices of children at play that had been the attraction.

Afterward Lindsay had thrust the episode out of her mind so resolutely that she had never once thought of it again. Now, however, the scene came back to her in vivid detail. She could all but hear the drone of honeybees flitting about, gathering pollen from her aunt's well-tended flower beds. Smell the wonderful sweet fragrance of jasmine as the sprinkler sprayed crystal-clear drops of moisture across lacy white flowers. See herself running toward the fence. The little girl who had been Lindsay wore shiny patent-leather shoes and a frilly white dress with a big ruffled organdy collar. A pink bow pulled her long, glossy black hair into a ponytail.

The grown-up Lindsay could still recall that child's acute disappointment when the fence proved to be too high to see over. Playmates in her young life were scarce. She had no brothers or sisters, and moving around so often because of Daddy's job made it hard to find and keep friends. Her parents loved and played with her, of course. But sometimes she yearned to be around people her own size who spoke her own language, for a change, instead of talking in Turkish or Siamese or Spanish.

Six-year-old Lindsay was almost positive she had found them. How disgusting not to be able to look across that fence and make sure!

Refusing to be thwarted, the determined little girl went in search of something to stand on. Near the rose trellis she found a bucket half filled with peat moss. Dumping out the crumbly planting mix, she toted the bucket over to the fence and turned it upside down. Then she climbed onto it and stretched up on tiptoe to see over the top of the fence.

It was an awfully long way down to the grass on the other side. Much farther than the drop to the ground on her own side. The bucket didn't feel as sturdy as it had looked, either. But she was up here now. Trying to ignore the creaks underfoot, Lindsay clung tightly to the tops of the weathered boards and studied the festive scene.

Balloons and crepe-paper streamers brightened the yard next door. Two long picnic tables had been set up on the deck. They were covered with cartoon-character tablecloths and piled with colorfully wrapped boxes. She counted fourteen paper cups and plates, with a little dish of candy anchoring the napkin at each place. Even without a cake and candles, Lindsay didn't have a bit of trouble recognizing a happy-birthday party when she saw one.

From the shouts echoing around the side of the house, she could tell that the party guests were playing hide-and-seek. Only two boys were visible from where she stood. They had run off from the others to duck down behind some scraggly bushes right underneath the fence.

"Hi!" Lindsay called down to them.

Someone suddenly roaring "BOO!" from behind a Frankenstein mask couldn't have prompted a more startled reaction. Both boys jerked to their feet and spun around. Their heads tilted up. Their mouths dropped open when they caught sight of her.

Lindsay thought they were very strange-looking children. Instead of having black hair and brown eyes like practically everybody else she had ever met, these boys had yellow hair and blue eyes. Big blue eyes, round with fright. From the quick, nervous glances they darted over their shoulders, Lindsay guessed they would have liked to run away. She figured the only reason they didn't was that neither of them wanted to act like a scaredy-cat in front of the other.

"Is that what you saw before, Erik?" one of them finally blurted.

The second boy's shirt was bright red. Lindsay noticed it particularly because the contrast between the vivid cloth and his pale cheeks was so great.

"No," he answered in a choked voice.

"You sure?"

Erik bobbed his head. "Yeah, Gunnar, I'm sure. That other — well, she was floaty. First she was there, and then she wasn't."

"Well, I think this one's a ghost too," Gunnar insisted stubbornly. "She's floating, all right. How else could she get clear up there on top of the fence?"

Lindsay had never heard such foolishness in all her life. Had she dared, she would have stamped her foot in aggravation. But she had a feeling the bucket wouldn't hold up to that sort of treatment.

"I'm not floating. I'm holding on," she loftily informed the two boys in the next yard. "Aren't you going to ask me to come to the party?"

They were all about the same age, but the idea of doing any such thing seemed to scare Gunnar stiff. He backed away, one unsteady step at a time. "Go away!" he commanded shakily. "Fly away and leave us alone!"

The boy called Erik was made of sterner stuff. A little color seeped back into his pale face as he gawked up at Lindsay. Edging closer to the fence, he shoved the floppy-looking yellow hair out of his eyes. "You can't fly away . . . can you?" he asked, curiosity seeming to win out over fright. "You aren't *really* —"

Couldn't he see she was a *girl?* "Not really *what?*" Lindsay demanded, so exasperated that she forgot about the rickety bucket and stamped her foot.

She never heard the boy's answer. The base of the bucket caved in at the first *whack* of her patent-leather shoe. Toppling over, it left Lindsay suspended from the top of the fence by her fingertips. A split second later she was flat on her back on the ground with the breath knocked out of her.

As if from a long distance away, Gunnar's horrified voice gasped, "I told you so! First she was there and then she wasn't. Just like you said that floaty —"

"Got you! You're it!" cried a new voice, a girl's this time.

Lindsay knew that even if she could find something else to stand on, it was too late now to learn what those stupid boys had been talking about. She picked herself up and fled.

"Sweetheart, what happened?" her mother asked when she had pelted back to the patio where her parents were having tea with Great-Aunt Felice.

"I fell down," Lindsay sobbed and let it go at that. It would have been too humiliating to admit that someone had mistaken her for a *ghost*. She allowed herself to be cuddled and fed a piece of cake — better, she felt sure, than the rotten birthday cake they'd be having next door. She told herself not even to think about the dumb, dumb, DUMB things those boys had said.

And she'd kept that resolve, Lindsay realized now. Not once in twenty years had she replayed that insulting, infuriating, *mystifying* incident in her mind or tried to figure out what had made the boys act so strange.

She'd never even thought of them again until this very minute when she'd walked over to the fence and gazed down.

The neighbors' yard looked much different today than it had back when she was a child. The bushes the boys had ducked behind had been replaced by ivy clustering thickly against the retaining wall. The picnic tables and party decorations had also vanished. Instead, Lindsay found herself eyeing scaffolding and drop cloths and buckets of paint.

The only person in view was a tall, broad-shouldered man standing on a ladder with his back to her. He was nailing a strip of ornamental molding to the balcony extending out from a second-story window. The ease and precision with which he swung the hammer gave the impression that he did that sort of thing all the time and did it very well. He would have to, Lindsay reflected. No ordinary workman would ever be given permission to tinker with a house like that.

As a freshman and sophomore in college she had seriously considered pursuing a career in architecture. In the end she had switched to other studies. Meanwhile, though, she received a thorough grounding in the types of houses Americans had been building and living in over the centuries. The house next door was an impressive example of Carpenter Gothic, the most fanciful of all Victorian architectural variations. At an educated guess, it had probably been built around the end of the Civil

War. Now it seemed to be receiving a complete face-lift.

Though younger by a quarter of a century, her own Queen Anne home could sure use some of that TLC, she thought with a tinge of envy. The workman handling the renovation seemed to know exactly what he was doing. Like herself, he was young — years under thirty. Unlike her, there was no doubt whatsoever that he enjoyed his work. He went at it with effortless competence, hammering happily away as if it were the best job in the world.

Lindsay found herself wishing she could see his face. What hair she could glimpse rimming the edge of his baseball cap looked very fair. The sleeves of his plaid shirt were rolled up above the elbows, displaying bronzed, well-muscled forearms dappled with golden fuzz.

With the shirt and cap he wore work boots and an ordinary pair of Levi's. They were dusty, a bit faded, and about as plain as a pair of pants could be. They certainly didn't have any of the upscale styling details that made the clothing in Denim Ala Mode so popular. And expensive.

Lindsay couldn't quite restrain a giggle. She had a hunch that if the man poised so capably on the ladder over there ever got a look at the price tags clipped to the jeans in the stores she managed, he'd probably laugh himself silly. Now that she thought of it, the notion of paying satin-and-lace prices for mass-produced denim seemed pretty ridiculous to her too.

The irrepressible sound of mirth rippling toward him on the late-afternoon breeze caused Erik Thorvaldsen to muff a stroke with his hammer. That seldom happened. Usually he grew so engrossed in his work that he could go on for hours, cheerfully blocking out anything that didn't have to do with the restoration of classic homes. But a whisper of instinct warned that this was no ordinary distraction.

The height of the ladder on which he was standing compensated for the fact that the Jensen yard was so much lower than the property on the other side of the wall. Slowly Erik turned his head. Feelings he couldn't even begin to explain rushed over him as for a long, long moment he stared straight across at the girl with the silky black hair and stunning brown eyes who'd been drifting in and out of his life for the past twenty years.

This time, was she real?

Chapter Two

She was beautiful. But was she real?

This young woman's face was uncannily like the one he'd glimpsed so often, but her hair was different. Instead of being shingled off even with her ears, a yard or so of glossy black silk drifted back across her shoulders.

The ripple of laughter, too, went a long way toward convincing Erik that the girl beyond the fence was no chimera. Something had evidently struck her funny; a smile danced across her lips. Her look-alike had never made a sound, and a sort of agonized hope was the only expression he had ever seen on her lovely face. Each time that hope faded to disappointment the moment he approached, as if she soon realized he wasn't the one she'd been longing to see. Then, before he could blink, she'd be gone. Vanished into thin air. Until the next time, when the identical scene would be enacted again.

Always in the same place. Back there at the gazebo. Why, after all these years, would she start wandering around the yard? It didn't make sense.

"Who you kiddin', Thorvaldsen?" he muttered under his breath. "Since when did things have to make sense for you to believe in them?"

Erik squeezed his eyes shut, giving her a chance to disappear if that was what she intended to do. When he opened them again, he was almost surprised to see her still there. But now her amused expression had been replaced by a look of alarm. He realized why a half second later when he felt the ladder wobble.

"Look out!" she cried.

The shock of seeing her had thrown Erik perilously off balance. Trying to regain his equilibrium, he made a desperate grab for the balcony. His hand caught a section of milled fretwork. Unfortunately the ornamental border had only been tacked into place. The thin piece of wood trim parted from its backing with a resonant *crack!* An instant later it was tumbling down on top of him.

Lindsay peered down in dismay. Man, ladder, tools, and ripped-off molding were tangled in an awkward heap on the ground. "Are — are you okay?"

Several dazed seconds passed before

Erik revived enough to start taking inventory. The jarring fall had temporarily knocked the breath out of him. But luckily it seemed that the snapping sounds he'd heard had been splintering wood instead of breaking bones.

Not that he still didn't have a few problems. Pain shot through his leg when he tried to pull it free, and an ominous screech of board against glass caused him to sag hastily back to the ground.

"I can't get up!"

Hearing the cry, Lindsay visualized compound fractures. "Don't try to move," she called back. "Lie perfectly still while I run inside and call an ambulance."

"Hold on! I'm not that badly hurt," he insisted. "My knee is strained, that's all. But I can't push free of the ladder. If I try to shift it from down here, it'll crash through that window."

"I'll come give you a hand."

"Thanks. Take the back way; it's quicker. Just follow the fence right down to the creek," he directed. "The bank isn't steep. You can swing around from one yard to another as easy as —"

"As falling off a ladder? Lie still till I get there."

Following the fenceline wasn't quite as

simple as he'd made it sound. Detouring around a brambly berry patch and skirting outflung tree limbs, Lindsay forged ahead until the ripple of fast-swirling water very close by made her pause cautiously.

Francis Creek, she remembered the banker calling it. Swollen from the past winter's rains, the current flashed along, fording rocks and pushing limbs and leaves downstream ahead of it. On the very edge of the bank, a round structure with a high domed roof supported by four lamentably weathered columns drooped over the water as if hoping to see a reflection in its depths.

A feeling of utter sadness invaded Lindsay's senses as she gazed toward the gazebo. It wasn't difficult to understand why the executor for Aunt Felice's estate had called it a derelict that should have been torn down years ago. The old summerhouse still reminded her of a carousel, but a forlorn one, whose steeds had long since galloped off to frolic on a happier merry-go-round.

She tore her eyes away, recalling guiltily that she was supposed to be on a mission of mercy. Wasting no more time, she grabbed the corner of the fence and swung herself nimbly into the next yard.

The rear half of the property was lush with fruit trees in blossom. Quickly she started back along the fence, which in a few yards was elevated to top a gradually rising retaining wall. Her heart gave a leap of anxiety when she ducked clear of the last of the trees and caught sight of the workman sprawled on the grass.

The ponderous ladder cries-crossed his body, pinning him down. Lindsay caught her breath when she saw the way his left leg was twisted through the rungs. That horrible thing was enough to crush his bones! Guilt for that wasted half minute spent beside the gazebo twinged at her. She should have been here, helping.

"Don't worry; I've come to the rescue." Lindsay forced a light tone into her voice as she dropped to her knees beside him and grabbed hold of one edge of the ladder.

She was so small and delicate, Erik thought in dismay. What could he have been thinking of, dragging her into a situation like this? "Look," he protested, feeling a trickle of perspiration plow through the dust on his forehead, "maybe you'd better not —"

He must be hurting something awful, yet he was worrying about her. At a time like this! Marveling at his generous spirit, Lindsay brushed aside his objection and tightened her grip on the rough wood. "I'm stronger than I look," she hushed him. "Think you can scoot out backward while I prop it up?"

She had the most stubborn little chin he'd ever seen. She wouldn't go away, Erik thought with certainty. He didn't want her to, not really. But he couldn't stand the thought of her hurting herself on his account, either. Still, her plan might work — if they both gave a thousand percent.

"Gonna try," he promised and put every ounce of concentration to work in making a quick escape.

Doing her best not to cave in under the strain of hoisting the ladder off him, Lindsay watched in awe as the young carpenter's muscles bunched and rippled and he succeeded in pulling himself free of the runged cage. Then he was up, standing shoulder to shoulder with her, accepting the lion's share of the weight as they pivoted the hefty wooden frame away from the windows.

Seconds later Lindsay realized how much the effort must have cost him. He had sunk down again, clasping his knee with both hands as thick, fair hair drooped across his bent forehead. Pain had siphoned the healthy bronze color right out of his cheeks. The sudden pallor jogged her memory. Long ago a small boy in a red shirt had turned white as a sheet when she called down to him from the top of that fence.

She bent over and picked up the baseball cap that he had lost during the fall, turning the warm cloth round and round with nervous fingers. Was this that same boy, grown older? He'd been so little and frightened then; she must have really scared him, popping up so unexpectedly. But they'd been children that time, and now they were grown. Why had the sight of her a few minutes earlier shaken him up so badly that he'd pitched headfirst off his ladder?

This was scarcely the time to quiz him about that, however. "Is — is anything broken?" she asked apprehensively. "Should I call the ambulance, after all?"

"No, of course not." Erik felt somewhat embarrassed to be acting like such a weakling. He quit rubbing his injured knee and accepted the hat she held out to him. "I wrenched this playing basketball in my teens." He offered a sheepish explanation. "Ever since, the least little bump makes it ache like the devil."

Men! Lindsay thought. If pitching twelve feet straight down to the hard ground was what he called the least little bump, she would certainly hate to watch him have a real accident!

The lowering sun sparked a dazzle of gold in his hair as he tilted his head back to put his hat on again. Lindsay could still recall how astonished she'd been that time when she'd looked over the fence at the two boys with their blue eyes and hair the color of freshly churned butter. Nowadays she had many blond friends. Even so, she had seldom encountered anyone so striking in appearance as this splendidly proportioned young Viking.

Though there were several questions she yearned to ask, Lindsay was too kindhearted to pester someone in pain. She started to turn away from him. "Guess I'd better be going."

"No, wait!" Erik forced himself to forget his throbbing knee while he sent a speculative gaze skimming her face. He hadn't been mistaken about the resemblance; the likeness between them was absolutely incredible. But this girl was full of life and bounce — and spunk. She could have hurt herself seriously, straining to haul that ladder off him, but it hadn't daunted her. Not for a minute.

Rashness like that always packed a penalty.

"Don't rush off," he coaxed. "I'd like a chance to thank my rescuer and to return the favor. You've picked up a couple of nasty splinters in your hand. They need to come out before they fester."

Lindsay looked down at her fingers in surprise. She *had* felt something gouge into her flesh when she grabbed that rough ladder, come to think of it. But imagine his being so observant.

Glancing up, she met his eyes again. "Any chance of furnishing an explanation along with the first aid?" she asked in a light tone. "Until you turned around and saw me, you seemed as at home on that ladder as Peter Jennings is behind a microphone. What happened to suddenly make you lose your balance?"

You'd never believe me in a hundred years, Erik thought. He shrugged. "I heard somebody laugh, and the sound startled me," he said, take-it-or-leave-it. "The woman who owned that house died not long ago; it's been standing empty ever since. I thought there might be a . . . trespasser . . . over there."

His eyes looked shuttered. Lindsay wondered what word he had substituted "trespasser" for and suspected that she knew. "Why would a 'trespasser' walk over to the fence and attract your attention?"

Persistent lady, Erik thought. But since curiosity was one of his own character traits, he could hardly fault her for seeking an answer, even though he had no intention of furnishing it.

He shrugged again. "Criminals aren't necessarily known for their high IQs."

Good point. In disgust Lindsay chalked one up to him. It might even have rung true had she not seen him squeeze his eyes shut after taking that first incredulous look at her. She had a hunch that if this young man with the high cheekbones and very stiff neck ever *really* spotted a trespasser, the prowler, not he, would be the one to land flat on the ground.

But he hadn't mistaken her for a trespasser. He'd thought she was somebody else. Some*thing* else, maybe. Looking back twenty years in time, she remembered how close to panic the two little boys had come at their first sight of her.

What was it about her that made the males of this town behave so weirdly?

Before she could push for some answers,

he turned away from her and stooped over to pick up his hammer.

Dismay caused Lindsay to abandon one line of questioning to blurt out another. "You don't mean to climb back up on that ladder *today*, do you?"

"No. It's quitting time." Erik tossed aside the broken piece of molding, counting his blessings that it was the thin wood that had shattered and not his leg. "I'll tackle it again tomorrow. Meanwhile, though, a good carpenter never leaves his tools lying around."

"Just be careful," Lindsay teased, retaliating for allowing herself to be sidetracked. "Next time you slip, there might not be a concerned trespasser looking over the fence to offer assistance."

He had a full, generous mouth. Under ordinary circumstances she suspected it might smile easily. It verged on a grin now. "Okay, okay," he conceded. "The minute I saw you, I knew you belonged to that house over there."

The expression struck her as odd. And peculiarly true. She *did* belong to the house, and it to her. If only she could stay!

That wasn't possible, worse luck. But it wasn't his problem. "*How* did you know?" she probed.

"Let's just say there's a family resemblance that won't quit." This wasn't a subject Erik wanted to discuss, but when she continued to stand there, hands on hips, he dredged up an old incident from his youth, hoping it would pacify her into dropping the whole subject.

"A friend of mine used to deliver papers on this block. The summer we were eleven, he fell off his bike and broke his leg. I took over his route for a couple of months to help him out. The first time I came around to collect, Miss da Silva told me to come into the parlor where she'd left her purse, so she could pay me. I saw those portraits over the mantel."

Lindsay couldn't deny that she looked a great deal like the subjects of those paintings. She couldn't understand why that would cause anyone to fall off a ladder, however. Still, she'd gotten him to open up a little. Maybe more than he'd intended to do.

Hoping to encourage further confidences, she gave him a friendly smile. "I'm Lindsay Dorsett," she introduced herself. "The portraits you saw are of my great-grandparents, Bartolomew and Luzia da Silva. Their daughter Felice was my great-aunt. She left me the house in her will. And you're — ?"

"Erik." He engulfed her hand in a firm clasp. "Good to meet you, Lindsay."

Erik! So her hunch had been right. He *was* one of the boys who'd been playing hide-and-seek in this yard the day of that long-ago birthday party! Lindsay's elated reflection merged with a sharp twinge of discomfort, however, as the carpenter's strong fingers curled around hers.

"Ouch! You're forgetting the splinters!"

Immediately he eased the pressure. "I'm sorry," he apologized, wondering about that quick flash of recognition when she'd heard his name. He had deliberately avoided telling her the rest of it. Why kick up a lot of old unpleasantness?

He dropped his eyes, looking down at her hand to conceal those giveaway thoughts. "That was clumsy of me," he added. "I know how painful those rough slivers of wood can be. Working around old houses the way I do, I'm always bristling with them myself."

His hand was tough. Hard and callused. A workman's hand. It felt good holding hers, warm and strong and competent. More than that — almost familiar.

"A regular porcupine?" Lindsay's tone was light, but the thought that had just struck her was troubling. She pushed it away. This feeling that she knew him was ridiculous. So was the way he was dodging giving anything away about himself.

He took her up on the porcupine quip. "Good description. Because of that, I'm the most experienced splinter remover in Humboldt County. Got a first-aid kit? I'll be glad to demonstrate."

"My aunt may have kept one in the house." Lindsay glanced over her shoulder at the fence separating the two properties. "Shall we go find out?"

Even as she extended the invitation, Lindsay thought how astounded her roommates would have been to hear it. She tended to be cautious around strangers. Never would she have dreamed of asking a chance-met city acquaintance up to her apartment. Now, though, she didn't hesitate. They weren't strangers — not really. Today was their second meeting. And both encounters had raised questions that only he could answer!

Erik firmly pointed her in the other direction when she turned to retrace her steps through the backyard. He most definitely wasn't eager to walk past the gazebo in her company. On the other hand, continuing their conversation suddenly seemed like a great idea. An ambitious scheme had begun forming in his mind. Felice da Silva had flatly refused to cooperate with the request he'd made one time, but Lindsay Dorsett was someone from his own generation. He wanted a favor from her, and he was hoping she wouldn't know enough about the family history to refuse without even hearing him out.

"We'll be better off using the front gate this time," he decreed, starting toward it himself. "With a hand full of splinters, you might lose your grip on the fence. No sense risking a spill in the creek, right?"

He was certainly making a big deal out of a few minor splinters. Almost as if he had seized on them as an excuse to prolong their association. But that suited her just fine. She had reasons of her own for wanting to spend a bit more time in this man's company, and not one of them had anything to do with the fact that he was so good-looking.

"Right!" she cheerfully agreed. He was limping a bit; she slowed down so as not to outdistance him. "Besides, the ground is sort of rocky and slick back there on the bank. Anyone with a tricky knee is lots safer using the sidewalk."

This time Erik wasn't able to restrain his

grin. He'd been right, he thought. This one was something else. The sassy, gutsy sort that could hold her own in any contest. He couldn't picture her wilting away, from grief or any other cause.

"Go ahead," he said in a brave tone. "I wouldn't want to hold you up, hobbling the way I do."

Lindsay almost giggled again. He was pulling the old "Don't worry about me; I'll be fine" martyr routine! She picked up the pace, sauntering on out to the sidewalk while he lagged behind to lock the gate.

Her grin faded abruptly as she caught sight of the Chevy long-bed pickup parked at the curb. Not very new, the fanciest thing about it was the neatly lettered legend across the door.

Erik Thorvaldsen, Classic Restorations, she read.

So that's why he hadn't introduced himself properly! He was on the other side of that feud her aunt's executor had told her about. Its roots stretched back into history, he'd said, the bitter enmity having begun long before his time. But it was still a potent force. To this very day, so much rancor lingered between the two families that Felice da Silva had made it a pointed part of her will.

What she'd been doing the past twenty minutes was consorting with the enemy, Lindsay warned herself. She probably ought to head out right now. Tell Mr. Erik Thorvaldsen that she could cope with her own splinters, thank you very much, and leave him standing here, wondering what had happened.

But as a businesswoman Lindsay knew how wise it was to learn your enemy's strengths and weaknesses. Information was a mighty weapon when it came to staying ahead of the competition. And this man could undoubtedly tell her plenty.

Hearing the scrape of his boot on the cement, she mustered a bright smile and turned. She glanced pointedly from the logo on the truck door to the partially refurbished house he'd been working on.

"I gather you own the company responsible for restoring that Carpenter Gothic."

It pleased Erik to hear her accord the antique home its proper designation. Females who referred to Victorian houses as "those crumbling old places" or who clapped their hands and squealed "How quaint!" never rated a second phone call from him.

He nodded. "I've been fascinated with classic houses since I was a little kid. It's been my lifelong ambition to keep these wonderful old places intact for future generations. The earliest ones here in Ferndale are nearly 150 years old. Severely as the 1906 quake shook the town, they came through it practically unscathed. It's my job to keep these buildings from being torn down and replaced with modern structures that wouldn't be half so sturdy or beautiful."

Lindsay was finding it hard to muster any acrimony against him. "Lucky you, to be able to work at the job you love!"

Erik found her tone sincere, even a trifle envious. "Aren't you fond of what you do for a living?"

"I thought I was." Lindsay gave a rueful shrug. "I enjoy tackling challenges, and I'm really proud of what I've accomplished so far in my career. I earn quite an impressive salary managing two up-to-date clothing boutiques in the city."

"So what's the problem?"

"I've begun to wonder whether the success I've achieved is worth everything I had to give up in exchange," she answered frankly. "Hobbies, weekends, trips abroad to visit my dad, any chance of maintaining a serious relationship — they all had to be sacrificed while I kept my nose to the grindstone. It's taken a solid case of tunnel vision to get as far up on the management ladder as I've climbed."

"You want to watch out for ladders," Erik warned, turning in at her driveway. "You just saw what can happen when they tip."

Lindsay laughed outright. What a good sport he was and how easy to talk with! "I've seen it already. Several close friends have found the pressure of staying on top too much to handle." She looked up at the tall, blond man limping along at her side. "The trouble is that in a fast-track job like mine there's no happy medium. You just keep working harder and harder, earning more and more, climbing higher and higher — or you topple off the ladder."

"Sounds like a rotten way to go through life," Erik growled. "What happens if you jump off voluntarily?"

"Well, if you leap sideways, you can take up where you left off with another firm. Possibly improve your chances for advancement and get a few more perks. But if you fall, you're back to square one." Lindsay wrinkled her nose. "At least I've been getting Sundays off lately, though I still bring home fact sheets with me to study on my day off. And I do make good money, though to be truthful most of it goes toward rent and car payments, and maintaining a wardrobe that keeps me one hop ahead of the trends. That's a must in my business."

Her brown eyes were wistful as she glanced at the plain, ordinary clothing worn by the man next to her. The well-washed cottons didn't have a bit of style, yet he looked marvelous in them. Same with his truck. It was serviceable — and probably paid for long ago! How lovely, she thought, being one's own boss.

But who could afford it?

"What I've managed to save wouldn't go far toward refurbishing this house," she admitted, gesturing toward the mansion she had just inherited. "I imagine Classic Restorations charges the earth to take an antique home in hand?"

"Depends." Erik shrugged. "From May to October I'm swamped with lucrative job offers all up and down the north coast. I generally accept summer contracts on the basis of their earning power. The customers get their money's worth — but it's a *lot* of money. Has to be. What I earn in the warm weather lets me spend the rest of the year fixing up places I'm really interested in for not much more than the joy of preserving them."

Lindsay admired his commonsensical approach to money. Earnings were important, but instead of ruling his existence, they paid for the sort of life-style he preferred and added to his self-confidence.

Her long hair swayed as she angled her head toward the house he'd been working to restore. "Since it isn't May yet, I assume that place is one you're fixing up for the pleasure of it. Is it your own home?"

"It belongs to my favorite aunt and uncle," Erik replied. "They've gone off with my parents for a few months, touring the country in a Winnebago. The restoration is my way of thanking them for providing a second home for me during the years I was growing up. My cousin Gunnar and I have been best friends all our lives. Until he joined the Air Force, I spent as much time at his house as at my own."

His cousin's name removed the last of Lindsay's doubts. Erik and Gunnar. Those were the two boys she had called down to from the top of the fence. She wondered which of them the party had been for.

"When's your birthday?" she asked impulsively.

Erik blinked in surprise, thinking how unpredictable she was. "October seventeenth," he answered, not minding her curiosity since it would give him a chance to do some asking of his own later on. "Next fall I'll be twenty-six. How about you?"

"I turned twenty-six last week," Lindsay replied. "I'm almost exactly six months older than you."

She would have expected Erik to shrug off the slight disparity in their ages. Instead, he looked pensive. "That's an odd coincidence."

"What's so coincidental about my being older than you?"

"Not just older, but exactly half a year. That was the same difference as —" In the nick of time Erik restrained his runaway tongue. "As another couple I know of," he finished lamely.

Lindsay felt a jab of annoyance. Why was he acting so cagey? Why not name the people he was talking about? It wasn't as if she'd know them, anyway.

It seemed that those questions, too, were destined to go unanswered. Frustrated when Erik pointedly transferred his attention to the house they were approaching, Lindsay swung away from him to stride briskly up the steps. Favoring his injured leg, her companion came on more slowly, taking the time to make an appreciative study of the double doors with their stained-glass insets.

"Nice." He ran his fingertips across a row of fishscale shingles beneath the ornate mailbox. "I love all the care that went into these elegant old Queen Annes. The builders took the time to treat every little detail with the importance it deserved."

Lindsay led the way inside with a catch in her throat. She'd have been better off sharing Ceci's scorn for old houses. That way it wouldn't hurt so much to think of having to part with this one. But every time her eye was caught by one of those intricate details Erik had commented on, she wanted to wrap the place up in her arms and never let it go.

Was that what Felice da Silva had expected when she made out her will? If so, Lindsay thought with a flash of anger, her great-aunt had been a hundred years behind the times, just like the house itself. Modern-day career women didn't live in obsolete mansions like this. Even if they wanted to, they couldn't afford *that,* either!

Tears prickled behind her eyelids. Fortunately Erik was studying the graceful spandrels arching above the dining-room entrance and failed to notice her distress. Lindsay drew a deep breath to wrestle her emotions under control.

"You're welcome to sit down and rest that knee, if you like. I'll see what I can find in the way of splinter-removing equipment."

"Fine." He threw the absent answer over his shoulder.

The place was magnificent, he thought, gazing up the dizzying heights of the spiral staircase before proceeding into the drawing room. As an intimidated young paper boy he hadn't stopped to do much gawking the only other time he'd set foot under this roof. Now he could see what he'd been missing. The da Silvas might have had their shortcomings, but they took excellent care of their property.

So far, at least. It didn't sound as if the new owner had much leisure to spare for home maintenance. All he'd had in mind when he walked through that door was to ask for her cooperation in solving an old mystery. Now another ambition — the desire to stay, to make this place his own — began to seethe in his soul.

That, of course, could cause some problems. His parents' generation and his own hadn't been much affected by the old vendetta. But naturally his great-uncle Olin considered this house the enemy stronghold. He contended that the good name of the Thorvaldsens had been sorely maligned by the original inhabitants of this house.

Even if the place changed hands, would he ever agree to come inside?

When Lindsay returned a few moments later, she found him studying the portraits of her great-grandparents. "Wonderful, aren't they?" She crossed the faded carpet to join him. "But just one more problem for me, I'm afraid. The size of those paintings would dwarf any normal-sized room. What on earth am I going to do with them when I sell this house?"

It had never taken Erik Thorvaldsen long to make the important decisions in his life, then act on them. "You're definitely selling?" he asked, ignoring her comments about the portraits and cutting straight to the heart of the matter. "That's wonderful! From my point of view, at least. I'd be delighted to take the house off your hands."

Chapter Three

"Thank you for offering," Lindsay said with a firm shake of her head. "But I'm afraid that's impossible."

Affronted, Erik turned to stare at her. "What's impossible about it?" he demanded. "I'll top any other bid you get for the place, and I won't complain about the renovation it'll take to put it back in top shape, either."

Business must be pretty good at Classic Restorations, Lindsay thought.

"You don't understand," she clarified the issue. "It isn't that I don't *want* to sell the house to you. It's that I *can't*. Legally. It's a condition of my great-aunt's will. If I should attempt to sell the place to anyone connected with the Thorvaldsen family, it'll be turned into a nautical museum to honor the age of sail."

"That's discrimination!" So Lindsay Dorsett *had* known about the feud. Erik glowered at her. Why had she asked him over here, then? "If I wanted to be nasty, I could take you to court."

"You could try." Lindsay was fascinated at the way irritation had drawn his thick, golden eyebrows together. "I think you'd probably just be wasting your time. Her executor said that Felice da Silva consulted a very canny lawyer before making out that Last Will and Testament. According to him, if she wanted to restrict what happened to the property she was leaving behind, that was her legal right." She tilted her head, staring up at him with interest. "He also told me something about a feud. What did my aunt have against the Thorvaldsens, anyway?"

"It's an old story." Erik forgot for a moment that it was an old story that urgently needed settling and that he'd come over here counting on persuading her to help him find some answers. "Besides, it could just as easily be asked what the Thorvaldsens had against the da Silvas."

By now Lindsay was seething with curiosity. "Did it have anything to do with why you fell off the ladder when you saw me?"

Ouch! "Sorry. You're way off base."

"How about ghosts?" The question popped out, unplanned. From the expression on his face, she'd hit pay dirt.

"Ghosts?" Erik wished he'd taken her up on that invitation to sit down. All of a sudden both his knees felt shaky. "Where'd you get a wild idea like that?"

"From you." A spark of deviltry danced in Lindsay's eyes. "Remember my mentioning that I'd been here once before? I was six years old that time we came to visit Aunt Felice. There was a birthday party going on in the yard next door. You and your cousin Gunnar were playing hide-and-seek back by the fence."

Erik sat down abruptly. He thought back to the day of Gunnar's sixth birthday. He hadn't turned six himself yet, so the events of that day were among his earliest memories. Certainly the most vivid. He studied the dark-haired young woman standing beneath the portraits of her ancestors. *Incredible,* he thought, not for the first time.

"You looked over the fence — didn't you?"

Lindsay nodded. "I was standing on my tiptoes, on a bucket. I thought for sure you'd be polite and invite me to the party. Instead, you turned white as a sheet and started babbling about ghosts. You said that you'd seen something 'floaty.' You'd told Gunnar about it earlier, something about, 'First she was there and then she wasn't.' He thought I was a ghost too."

He remembered. Oh, how he remembered! Looking up and seeing her there came as a terrible shock after what had happened that morning. But he'd just about convinced himself that the little girl clinging to the top of the fence was a real person when she suddenly disappeared too.

"Where did you go?"

"The bucket caved in. I fell down." Lindsay swallowed her simmering excitement. He looked upset. Stunned! If she could just squeeze some answers out of him before he got a grip on himself again. . . . "Tell me about the ghost you saw."

"You wouldn't believe me."

"Does it sound like I'm doubting your word? What did she look like?"

"You're kidding, right?"

For a minute Lindsay just stared at him in bewilderment. Then some whisper of intuition made her turn and look up at the portraits.

"You said . . . something about a family resemblance."

"Yeah," Erik drawled. "A beaut. Cut your hair, and you'd be a dead ringer for Renae da Silva."

Lindsay sagged back against the mantel, grateful for its solid support. "Renae! Felice's younger sister? But, Erik, you couldn't have known her. She died . . . young."

She thought he was crazy, Erik realized. And she hadn't heard the half of it yet!

He grimaced. As a kid he had learned to keep those eerie incidents to himself for fear of being ridiculed by his brothers and friends. Gunnar was the only one he'd ever told about the phenomena he witnessed every time he went near the gazebo. His cousin had never seen anything himself, though. Erik had soon learned to keep his mouth shut and do his wondering in private.

But now, regardless of the cost, he had to speak up. To secure her help, he'd have to convince Lindsay that he was telling the truth. Get her on his side. Not an easy task in the best of circumstances, considering he was a Thorvaldsen and she a da Silva. The use of the term "dead ringer" sure hadn't been a tactful start.

Almost holding her breath, Lindsay waited for an answer from the tall, broad-shouldered man with the memories trapped in his serious blue eyes. What was he hiding?

"You're right," he agreed at last. "Renae da Silva died on March 28, 1926, just three days before her twenty-second birthday. But I've been . . . bumping into her, you might say, ever since I was five years old. Every time I've gone near the gazebo."

Lindsay shivered, remembering the sad emanations she'd felt just walking past the old summerhouse. "That place! Anyone would imagine things down there, it's so creepy."

"I know the difference between imagining something and seeing it with my own eyes."

His stiff tone should have warned Lindsay, but it didn't register right away. "It was forlorn. Melancholy," she added. "That splintery old building should have been torn down decades ago!"

"No!" The suggestion jolted Erik's annoyance into alarm. "You wouldn't say that if you knew the background of the place."

Another shudder rippled up her spine. "I'm not sure I want to hear it."

"Oh, I get it," he scoffed. "You're delighted to know all about the pleasant parts of your heritage; but when it comes to the skeletons in the closet —"

"Whose closet — yours or mine?"

Her spirited demand came as a relief to Erik. He'd been afraid she was going to wimp out on him. "Both closets," he taunted. "There's a connection between us, Lindsay Dorsett. Don't you want to know what the feud was all about? Why your family despised my family so thoroughly that your great-aunt threatened to turn this house into a museum rather than allow a Thorvaldsen to have it?"

If she didn't find out, she'd spend the rest of her life wondering about it, Lindsay knew. "All right," she snapped. "Tell me about it."

Deliberately Erik turned away. He needed time to set the scene. Persuade her to do what he wanted. What had happened just now told him she couldn't resist a challenge. He'd have to let her see how intriguing the puzzle was, then bait the hook with a dare.

"Come over here where the light is better," he said, moving toward the French doors. "I'll take those splinters out, and then I have to get on home and change. I promised to be somewhere tonight, and I never go back on my word."

"What about your word to me?" she protested, stalking angrily after him. "You were going to tell me about the skeletons in the closet."

"Closets." With studied nonchalance,

Erik lifted her small, soft hand and probed deftly at a sliver of wood trapped under the skin. "I wouldn't mind filling you in on a tarnished episode in our family history — both families, I'm speaking of, you understand — when I've got the time. Let's see. Did you still plan on being in Ferndale on Sunday?"

"*Sunday!* That's nearly a whole week off!"

"Up to you, of course." Erik removed the second splinter, then returned the needle and tweezers with the air of a weary surgeon laying down his scalpel after performing a major operation. "My schedule's pretty demanding. That's the earliest I can take time out to sit around and chat. Unless — You could come along tonight, I suppose."

"Come along where?"

"To dinner. My cousin and her fiancé are launching a new restaurant. I promised to show up as a token of family solidarity. Together, you and I could provide twice as much moral support. That is, if you don't mind breaking bread with a Thorvaldsen."

Lindsay had been well acquainted with reverse psychology since she was a child. Who did this big, blond Viking think he was kidding?

"I could probably bear up under the disgrace," she allowed, as poker-faced as he. "If I go, I get the whole story? Feud, ghost, skeletons, and all?"

"Yup." Erik had a good idea of how she'd gotten so far up on the management ladder. Push-push-push. Stepping out onto the patio, he glanced at his serviceable old work watch. "Seven-thirty?"

"I'll be ready."

Erik restrained a grin as he strode around front. He'd whetted her appetite to know more. Now all he had to do was pull the carrot along, nice and slow.

When he reached the sidewalk, he looked back at the turreted Queen Anne. Lindsay Dorsett was exactly the sort of partner he needed to see the endeavor through. A tenacious woman with the gritty staying power to reach her goal regardless of how many obstacles were in her way.

She'd told the truth about being stronger than she looked, he admitted. With a dainty frame like hers, a lot of it had to be strength of spirit. Inner drive was a quality he recognized, being blessed with plenty of it himself. Resolutely he pushed away the memory of her set, stubborn jaw as she'd tugged and strained to hoist that ladder off him.

Just as well she didn't plan on being in town long. Erik felt a smile soften the hard angles of his face, remembering the way she'd stood her ground and challenged him to answer her questions. But his mirth quickly faded. She didn't belong here. She didn't know a single thing about the suspicion and animosity that bound their opposing heritages together while keeping them at arms' length.

Unfortunately, there was no way to gain her help without opening up the whole can of worms. Maybe the story he had to tell would keep her from repeating her suggestion about tearing down the gazebo. Dismantling it would be the final indignity in a two-family saga that already contained too much melodrama.

That was the first thing anyone she sold the place to would think of doing, worse luck. But it couldn't be allowed to happen. Putting his truck in gear, Erik mulled over the problem of circumventing Felice da Silva's will.

Lindsay pointed the 'Vette in the direction of the grocery store. Annoyingly, thoughts of Erik Thorvaldsen intruded, interfering with her attempts to compile a mental list of supplies.

It wasn't just his good looks that made him hard to forget. The recollection that recurred to her most often was his steadfast courage. That fall would have put most people in the hospital, but even crushed by the weight of the ladder, his main concern had been that she not hurt herself while trying to help him.

There was something almost magnetic about the way she'd felt drawn to him. At first, anyway. Before he'd jumped in so quickly with a bid to buy the house that she'd wondered whether there might be oil on the property, or something. The next thing she knew, he was hinting about skeletons in the closet — closets — and laying down the law to her about not tearing down the old gazebo.

Who did he think he was, anyway?

The bare minimum of supplies she purchased at the market looked lost on the shelves of the vast pantry. They were as out of place as she herself was in this enormous mansion, Lindsay reflected. The house had been built for a large, old-fashioned family. Back at the turn of the century, her great-grandparents had had a whole corps of servants to handle the cooking and cleaning and to keep an acre of grounds manicured.

But people didn't live that way anymore, Lindsay thought crossly. The modern-day world was a practical place.

Upstairs she chose a room for herself from among the eight spacious bedchambers on the second floor. Then, aware that Erik would soon be calling for her, she hurried to bathe and change. A cedar-lined hall closet produced fresh bed linen as well as heaps of elegant towels. She had just encased fluffy pillows in lavender-scented percale when a thud from the metal knocker downstairs announced her visitor.

Until she saw him standing on her doorstep, Lindsay didn't realize how apprehensive she'd been that Erik might have been more seriously injured than he'd let on earlier. To her relief, the limp had now disappeared. He looked freshly scrubbed, bursting with vital good health, and very, very handsome.

"Hi," she said a trifle breathlessly. "You're right on time. It will take only a second to get my jacket."

Erik Thorvaldsen was never going to be the sort of man who'd worry about what was "in" and what was "out," Lindsay thought. Not in the job he worked at or the vehicle he drove, and most definitely not in the clothes he wore. The outfit he had on tonight was neither fashionable nor unfashionable — merely timeless. His silky, dove-gray shirt had long, full sleeves that buttoned at the wrists. Over it, he wore a suede vest embroidered with silver thread. Like it, his trousers were charcoal, sharply creased. The leather of his black Justin boots had been buffed to a high sheen.

He looked like a fair-haired charro.

What a knockout! Erik eyed the ebony cloud hanging halfway down Lindsay's back as she swung away. In the scarlet chiffon dress with its fitted bodice and flaring, boot-length skirt she looked vibrantly alive.

How could he have confused her with Renae for even a moment?

The sharp, sudden pull of attraction appalled him. He didn't want to be drawn to Lindsay Dorsett. In the past year he'd started to hanker for a wife and family of his own and had begun to keep an eye out for the right girl — a pretty blonde whose background was similar to his own, he assumed she'd be, like the women his three brothers had married.

But however *that* hope turned out, he had no intention of becoming personally involved with the last of the da Silvas. One liaison between their families had been intense enough to kindle a blaze of enmity that still hadn't smoldered out seven decades later. Only a lunatic would risk a second brush with that sort of fate.

Erik reminded himself that he was a man with his head on straight and a long-cherished goal. What he wanted from Lindsay Dorsett was her help in fulfilling it. All he asked was a few hours of her time to look for some old letters. Afterward she was welcome to jump right back into her fast-lane stress machine again.

In fact, Erik told himself, the sooner she went, the better.

With a light step Lindsay walked out to the curb. The reason she felt so pleased to see Erik, she assured herself, was that she could hardly wait to hear what he had to tell her about her family background. After all, she thought, when families have shared a feud, they were bound to have some insights about each other that nobody else knew.

She had a feeling that she'd been set up, though. He could just as easily have sketched out the information back there in the front parlor underneath her ancestors' portraits. But he'd made it a take-it-or-leave-it proposition: Come along tonight, or wait until Sunday. And Sunday, she'd be back in the city already.

Some of the exuberance went out of her stride at this reminder of how short their acquaintanceship was destined to be. Lindsay couldn't understand why it should have mattered. It wasn't as if they had anything in common.

Her place was in San Francisco. He belonged here in Ferndale.

She had a future to build for herself. His career was wrapped up in the past, inextricably bound to the antique houses he restored.

She had a Butterfat mansion to sell. He wasn't eligible to buy it.

As they approached the outskirts of the town, the stately Victorian dwellings were spaced farther apart. Lindsay gazed with interest at the gabled Gothic Revival dating from the 1870s when Erik turned in at its driveway and shoehorned his truck into a parking space.

An ornate sign placed in the middle of the lawn announced *Filini's North*. The house-turned-restaurant looked mistily romantic in the graying twilight. Its spotless ivory paint and the pristine condition of the decorative trim testified to recent, expert restoration.

"Your work?" Lindsay inquired as together they climbed the front steps.

Erik shrugged modestly. "Early wedding present."

Inside they were greeted by a tall young woman with sunshiny hair and eyes the same Nordic blue shade as Erik's. The unusual dress she wore appeared to be very nearly as old as the house.

With an excited smile Marta dropped the stack of menus she had been holding and hurried forward to hug her cousin. "Have a look at the final results," she invited elatedly. "Doesn't it look magnificent with the chandeliers lit and everything sparkling?"

"Superb. And you're every bit as sparkly as this high-class eating establishment," Erik teased, drawing Lindsay forward to perform introductions. "What sort of getup is that you have on?"

Marta twirled to give them the full effect of her floor-length ensemble. The narrow skirt with its modest train and matching, off-centered bolero were fashioned from a thin, lavender crepe. Fascinated, Lindsay noticed that bands of the same material edged the high collar of the lacy white long-sleeved blouse.

"I found it up in Gran's attic," Marta

confided. "It belonged to *her* gran, I think. A note pinned to the sheet swathing it said it was worn to some function in 1901. These days clothes all seem to be made with cookie cutters. I wanted something unique to wear when welcoming our customers, something that would also match the spirit of the house. This was perfect. But Gran's gran was slimmer than I am. I can hardly breathe!"

"Back at the turn of the century, eighteen-inch waists were considered the feminine ideal," Lindsay explained the tight fit. "Even women with hourglass figures were laced into whalebone corsets to make their waists as small as possible. I guess that must have motivated them not to eat."

"It's a wonder everyone back then wasn't anorexic!"

Marta picked up a pair of menus and escorted them down the house's central hall past several large rooms, all newly redecorated to cater to the restaurant's clientele, to an intimate dining salon. As Erik and Lindsay were being seated, a woman at a nearby table complimented Marta's costume and asked where she had bought it. She seemed disappointed to hear that the dress was a family heirloom, not available in stores.

"Old-fashioned styles must be on the verge of making a comeback," Marta said. "That's the second customer to positively drool over this dress tonight. The first woman offered to buy it right off my back."

"The name of this place rings a bell," Lindsay remarked after Marta had returned to her hostessing duties and a tuxedo-clad young man had filled their cut-glass stemware with a mellow Tuscan wine. "There's a famous Filini's on Fisherman's Wharf in San Francisco. Is Marta's fiancé related to them?"

Erik nodded. "The owners' son. Tony and his twin sister, Theresa, got their early training right there in Mama and Papa Filini's kitchen. Later, they both attended the Culinary Institute of America, in Hyde Park, New York."

"Sounds like we're in for a three-star dining experience. But how odd that the Filini family would choose a small place like Ferndale to branch out in."

"The Filini family had nothing to do with it," Erik confided. "Tony and Theresa were scheduled to take over the original restaurant a few years from now, when their parents got ready to retire. Then last winter Tony made a trip north. He fell in love with Marta and the redwoods country at the same time."

"Hence a change of plan?"

"One of those life-style turnarounds they call 'downshifting.' Tony's parents hit the ceiling, and Marta's folks went up in smoke. She had been chief accountant for an important firm in Eureka until she resigned her position to team up with Tony. Hostessing in a restaurant was a terrible comedown, in her parents' viewpoint." Erik helped himself to a crisp breadstick. "Things are finally starting to work out, I think. Both sides have started talking again. By September both families will probably be reconciled to becoming in-laws — even if they still don't speak the same language at home or attend the same church."

Lindsay wondered if he had stressed this point accidentally or whether he was leading up to something. "The same sort of ethnic disparity wouldn't have led to problems between our families by any chance, would it?"

Smart woman, Erik thought. *No need to draw pictures for her.* He grinned. "Back in the early 1920s someone here in town suggested that they change their names from Thorvaldsen and da Silva to

Montague and Capulet."

Lindsay saw at once what the feud must have concerned. "As in kin to Romeo and Juliet? Don't tell me our bloodlines produced a pair of star-crossed lovers!"

"That's exactly what they were," Erik said in dead seriousness. "Maybe in time the families would have become resigned to the match, but the way things worked out — Well, it was a disaster from the start. They could hardly have been more different. Portuguese and Danish. Dark and fair. Seafarer and dairy farmer. Catholic and Protestant. The only thing they had in common was a fence."

"The fence I looked over today?"

"Your old family home lay on one side," Erik acknowledged her guess, "while the Butterfat mansion on the other side belonged to the Jensens. My great-grandmother and Mrs. Jensen were sisters. Like me, Nils Thorvaldsen spent a big part of his growing-up years visiting kinfolk in that house. Kinfolk . . . and the girl next door."

"Renae?"

His eyes studied her face for a long minute. He seemed to be picturing another young woman, the one she so closely resembled.

"Yes, Renae." For the very first time he

began to understand the passionate attachment his great-uncle had felt. Thrusting the uncomfortable thought aside, he went on. "I was in my middle teens by the time I got curious enough to start digging into that old story. By then Helga Jensen was quite an old lady, but at the time I'm talking about she was just a young girl, a contemporary of theirs. She told me that her cousin Nils and Renae da Silva fell madly in love the first time they set eyes on each other. They couldn't have been more than five or six years old when that happened."

"That sounds pretty far-fetched," Lindsay remarked. "Usually little boys and girls don't much care for each other."

"There was never anything 'usual' about the relationship between Nils and Renae. According to Helga, it was one of those 'written in the stars' things," Erik insisted in a serious tone. "Being personally involved in a weird sort of way, I did a lot of digging to find out all I could. Everyone who had known Nils and Renae told me the same thing. Even Olin, Nils's brother."

The mention of his great-uncle gave Erik an uncomfortable twinge of guilt. That afternoon he had driven straight from Lindsay's house to the old man's large, modern dairy farm, and sat down with him for a strategy session. The notion of paying Felice da Silva back for decades' worth of snubs had appealed to Olin. Erik had followed his advice. Now the steady gaze of the girl across the table made him question his hasty action. But it was too late to back out.

"They all insisted that Nils and Renae were unbelievably devoted friends who weren't really happy unless they could be together," he hastily continued. "The gazebo down by the creek was their own special playhouse. They spent at least part of every day there, under the watchful eye of nursemaids whose duty it was to make sure nobody fell in the water or got sick from too many green apples."

"Sounds like an idyllic childhood."

"I think it was," Erik thoughtfully agreed. "Both families had plenty of household help, and before the First World War, Captain and Mrs. da Silva traveled a great deal. They went to the Orient and South America, as well as to Europe. Nils wasn't very strong as a kid. His mother coddled him and let him stay in town with her sister, rather than having to come straight home from school to help with the farm chores."

Lindsay ate a few bites of her salad. Delicious as it was, she couldn't seem to work up too much interest in the food. "The gazebo keeps coming into this," she murmured. "You said you saw . . . something . . . whenever you went near it."

"I saw *Renae*," Erik insisted. "Time and again the same thing happened. She'd come out of nowhere the minute I approached, then sort of dissolve into a mist of disappointment as soon as I started up the steps."

The story was ridiculous. Lindsay could just about picture another woman's reaction if her date took her out to dinner and spun her a wild tale like this. But she wasn't any other woman. She was a da Silva, by blood. And she had felt a terrible sadness this afternoon just as soon as she'd neared the summerhouse.

"Why?" she probed to the heart of the matter. "Why do you think this happened to you?"

Instead of giving her a direct answer, Erik removed a snapshot from his vest pocket and passed it across the table. Lindsay focused on the sepia-toned photograph of a young man standing beside an old-fashioned car. It wasn't just the car that was old-fashioned, she noticed. So was the odd part in the youth's hair, his high shirt collar, and the cap in his hand.

But his face was very, very familiar.

"What did you do, visit one of those studios where you can get your picture taken using lots of old-time props?" she asked with an uneasy laugh.

"Look on the back."

With a feeling of foreboding, Lindsay turned the photo over. *Nils with Papa's new car, July, 1923,* was written in faded but still-legible ink.

"The da Silvas weren't the only ones with a strong family resemblance among the generations." Erik said, tucking the photo away again. "From childhood on, I must have looked much like my great-uncle Nils did at the same age. I finally came to the conclusion that that was why Renae would run out to meet me each time. She was waiting for Nils. She's still waiting."

"You mean he — he *jilted* her?"

Lindsay's quick indignation spurred a similar response from Erik. "*Your* family said he jilted her. That's what the feud was all about. The da Silvas tried for years to keep Renae and Nils apart. They took her on a grand tour, encouraged her to marry somebody else — Nothing worked. I don't believe anything short of utter calamity ever would have succeeded in breaking up that relationship."

"But I gather that something did."

Erik forced himself to calm down. It was important to convince Lindsay, not browbeat her. If he was ever to find out the truth and make Olin's last years content, he needed her cooperation.

"Nils was a lot like me in temperament as well as appearance," he said in a quieter tone. "He hated cows but loved working with wood. Some of the pieces of furniture he made are family heirlooms. He was good. Really good. Unfortunately, he was also the oldest son. After he got into his teens, his father started leaning on him to put the chisel aside and take an interest in the family herd. Nils resisted. It was a battle of two strong-willed people all the way."

Lindsay could sympathize with Nils. It sounded as if he were a square peg, being shoved against his will into a round hole. "What about Renae?" she asked.

"Her parents began putting a lot of pressure on her to marry a man they felt would make an excellent son-in-law," Erik said. "Elidio Vargas was thirty. Sophisticated, wealthy, a ship owner of Portuguese extraction. He proposed to Renae on her eighteenth birthday. An eavesdropping servant spread the word around town when she turned him down flat. You can imagine how stunned her parents were when she announced that the only man she would ever marry was the seventeen-year-old son of a dairy farmer. She'd been in love with Nils all her life, Renae said. She intended to go right on being in love with him until the end of time."

"I don't suppose the Thorvaldsens were any more pleased to hear that than the da Silvas were."

"Hardly," Erik said, pleased and a little surprised that she was willing to consider the story from both sides' point of view. "Nils was shipped off to Denmark for the summer, with orders to help on his grandparents' farm and to transfer his affections to a nice Danish girl. The da Silvas packed up their whole family and weighed anchor for Europe. But the only Danish girl Nils even smiled at was the statue of the Little Mermaid in Copenhagen harbor. And neither a grand tour of the Continent nor the steamer trunks full of extravagant clothes Helga said she brought home from Paris and Rome succeeded in making Renae change her mind."

Erik had told the story of their ancestors

between bites of Chicken Marengo. Any other time, he thought, he would have enjoyed every mouthful of the superb entree prepared by Tony Filini. But for all he could recall, he might have been eating Chicken McNuggets. Now he paused while their coffee cups were filled, then recapped the end of the tragic tale over wedges of sinfully rich cheesecake.

"After both families returned to town, Renae and Nils were forbidden to meet. But Renae's sister Felice and Nils's brother Olin helped them find ways to be together. Helga Jensen had a shrewd idea that the coconspirators had a thing going too. I don't know if that was true or not. I can only tell you that after Nils left, they became bitter enemies and never spoke to each other again."

Lindsay wondered if that was the reason Felice had never married. Had she, like Renae, been madly in love with a Thorvaldsen?

She put down her fork, wishing she could have done justice to the excellent dinner. "Nils went away? Of his own free will?"

"Of his own free will and with Renae's connivance," Erik amazed her by saying. "She's the one who heard about a master furniture craftsman somewhere in the Midwest who was willing to take on a talented apprentice. Nils and his father were constantly at each other's throats by the summer of 1924. He hadn't turned twenty yet. Since there was no way they could be married without their parents' permission until they turned twenty-one, Renae urged him to accept the offer to learn his chosen profession with a master. They had already weathered one long separation, she said. This time it would be to their benefit. If his apprenticeship went well, he'd have an excellent job, and they'd be able to start their married life with a prosperous future to look forward to."

"That sounds sensible. In 1924 a girl from a wealthy family wouldn't have had any job training of her own. She'd be counting on her husband to earn the living." Lindsay took a deep breath, as though bracing herself for the bad news she felt sure was coming. "You said Nils left. Then what happened?"

"That's where the story ends," Erik replied. "All I can tell you for sure is that he never came back."

Chapter Four

Lindsay awoke to a flood of sunshine. Dancing light beamed across her bed, quilting it with a warm, golden glow.

She sat up, blinking to get her bearings in the unfamiliar room. The previous afternoon she had been in a hurry to change and bathe and choose a place to sleep. It was color, her own favorite colors, that had drawn her to this spacious corner bedchamber. Now, along with blues and greens and ivories, fanciful details delighted her eye. Stained-glass diamonds inset into side windows invited rainbows to come in and play. The crystal closet door-pull fashioned in the shape of a sphinx hinted at the 1920s craze for anything Egyptian. The large Art Deco mirror on the far wall, a molded sheaf of calla lilies adorning one corner, provided another vivid reminder of the flapper era.

Glimpsing swaying tree shadows in the glass while preparing for bed the evening before, Lindsay supposed that the mirror had been positioned to pick up the beauty of the out-of-doors and draw it into the room. Focusing now on the reflected scene, she saw that she had guessed right. Partially. Along with bits of garden and snatches of sky, the rounded dome of a gazebo also floated in the glass. The occupant of the bed would be able to see its airy reflection the instant she opened her eyes each morning.

She didn't need to be told whose room this once was. The gazebo had been Renae's own special place. Hers and Nils's. Even from up here on the second floor, Renae would have been able to keep an eye out for the boy she loved. As soon as he swung round the fence from the yard next door, she would have hurried down to meet him.

Hastily Lindsay yanked the gauzy curtains shut to blot out the scene. Just thinking about the two young lovers made her throat ache with unshed tears. They had been a fairy-tale pair, but unfortunately nobody could say what had happened to Prince Charming. So far as anyone knew, Nils had simply gone away and never come back.

Last night in the restaurant as they lingered over coffee, Erik had raised his stunning blue eyes to hers and said that, like

83

Renae, he had been waiting too. Waiting for her to come home to Ferndale to help him resolve that decades-old mystery.

"Helga and Olin both told me the same thing: that at the end of September, 1924, Nils told Renae good-bye and boarded an eastbound train."

"They must have known where he was headed."

"To Omaha." Erik looked disgruntled. "That would have automatically been the first part of the journey for anyone en route to the Midwest from northern California. There was a huge rail terminal there where passengers changed trains to continue on to hundreds of other destinations. But Nils and Olin had quarreled bitterly about his leaving. He never told his brother where he was bound. In fact, he severed his relationship with the entire Thorvaldsen family when he got on that train."

"Oh, but surely he must have kept in touch with Renae!"

"That was Helga's theory," Erik agreed. "According to her, Renae was her usual self during the fall and winter after Nils left. She went around with a happy look on her face, just as though she were convinced they'd soon be reunited."

"I'll bet they wrote back and forth every single day."

"It sounds logical. But right around the time of Renae's twenty-first birthday everything changed." That was the end of March 1925, Erik said. "Though she acted anxious and tense, Renae managed to hold her head up and pretend there was nothing wrong for a few months after that. But when Nils's twenty-first birthday passed and he still didn't come home, she must have accepted the fact that something was seriously wrong. She started losing weight. Helga's room was right across from hers in the next house. She said Renae sat up half the night reading because she couldn't sleep. She also began spending all day, every day, down at the gazebo."

"Because if he came back anywhere, he'd come back there?"

"That was probably her one hope," Erik agreed. "Her family believed Nils had jilted her. Renae's little brother started fights on the playground with Nils's youngest brother. The mothers didn't speak if they happened to attend the same charity bazaar. Sometime close to the holidays, Felice and Olin got into a screaming match in the post office."

"By this time the whole town must have

been taking sides."

Erik nodded. "They must have said some horrible things to each other. Unforgivable things. Felice claimed that Renae was wasting away with grief. Olin said it was her own fault. That she'd dreamed up this bright idea of sending his brother back East to study instead of staying on the farm where he belonged. But neither of them or anyone else really knew what had happened."

Lindsay had given up all pretense of trying to drink her coffee. "Do you mean to tell me that no one *ever* heard from Nils again?"

"Not a word. It was as if he had vanished off the face of the earth."

"And Renae?"

"She spent every waking moment at the gazebo." Knowing her heart had gone out to that other girl, Erik reached across the table and took Lindsay's hand. "You've seen the place. Back then I don't suppose it tilted over the creek the way it does today. Maybe the roof didn't leak, either. Still, it wasn't much protection against the elements, and winters here tend to be wet and chilly. Pneumonia weather."

Lindsay clung to the warm comfort of his hand. "She got sick? Oh, poor kid!"

More than once it had occurred to Erik that what had happened to Renae was her own fault. She could have had a rich, rewarding life as the wife of Elidio Vargas or one of her other suitors. But she hadn't seemed able to work through her misery. With a twinge he wondered whether anyone would ever love him that much. It seemed unlikely. The 1920s were more than another time; they were almost a different world.

"That's right," he answered. "Helga told me about the wicked cough she picked up. Chills and fever followed."

"They had already lost three of their children," Lindsay whispered, picturing the anguish her great-grandparents had suffered for Renae's sake.

"They got a specialist up from the city. Hired a live-in nurse to make sure she had the best of care. She seemed to be pulling out of it —" Erik paused to clear his throat, then continued in a gruff voice laden with emotion. "Afterward they decided she must have been delirious when she got up in the middle of the night and made her way barefoot down to the gazebo. Next morning she was found there, huddled on the bench in her nightgown. At first they were hopeful that she'd only fallen asleep. . . ."

"But she'd died, hadn't she?" Lindsay's eyes glistened with tears. "Died waiting for Nils!"

"Yes, she died." There was challenge in the look Erik gave her. "I think she's still waiting."

With a shiver Lindsay snatched her hand away. Was it possible? He sounded convinced, but —

"Don't you have *any* idea of where Nils went or why he failed to return?"

He'd never get a better opening than that, Erik decided. "Not a clue. It's possible, though, that we might be able to find out."

"After all this time? How?"

At least she hadn't rejected the notion out of hand. She hadn't called him crazy, either, though Erik felt sure that a lot of people would have had some serious doubts about his mental stability by now.

He leaned forward, making the most of his chance. "We both agreed that Nils must have written to Renae for at least a few months after leaving California, right? If we can find those letters, we might be able to trace him by starting with the return address on them."

"Maybe." It was such a long time ago.

But if people could trace their family trees back through the centuries, Lindsay didn't see why this project shouldn't be possible. "Have you tried?"

"Not yet. Each of our families played an equal role in that old tragedy," Erik reminded her. "I'm convinced it will take a da Silva and a Thorvaldsen working together to ferret out the truth."

Lindsay realized now what he'd been getting at. If those letters had been preserved, they would be in the da Silva house. "Good thinking," she said. "Did you talk to my great-aunt about this?"

"Get real!" he said in disgust. "She *hated* the Thorvaldsens!"

Remembering Felice's will, Lindsay looked down at the tablecloth in embarrassment. "I guess hatred makes people act as irrationally as fever does."

On the one occasion he'd made an effort to explain his idea to Felice da Silva, she had accused the Thorvaldsens of bringing bad luck to her family and slammed the door in his face.

But his great-uncle Olin was every bit as resentful, Erik said. "He still feels guilty as sin about quarreling with Nils before he left. He inherited the family dairy farm instead of his older brother, you see, and almost all his life he's had to wonder whether things wouldn't have been different if he'd stayed out of the dispute."

"Imagine the two of them living with regrets for nearly seventy years!"

"There's not much time left. Olin's old, Lindsay," Erik said in distress. "If I'm to find a way to ease his mind, I can't let it go any longer. Will you help?"

"Absolutely." She could spare a few days to help bring an old family feud to a close, Lindsay told herself. "What do you want me to do?"

Looking relieved, Erik said that if her family was anything like his, they never threw anything away.

"Try to find those letters. He took the train east to serve an apprenticeship with an established furniture maker. That man wouldn't still be alive, of course, but his sons or grandsons might be. If Nils was on the payroll, there'd likely be records. Possibly a forwarding address."

Erik's idea had sounded logical. Simple, even. Pledging her support, Lindsay had pictured herself opening the drawer of a nightstand and pulling out a stack of letters tied with faded blue ribbon.

In reality, following through was nowhere near so easy. Anything personal had long since been cleared out of Renae's old room. Even the bookshelves were empty. Except for the period decor, it could have been any room, in any anonymous house, anywhere!

She thought it likely that after Renae's death, Bartolomew and Luzia had arranged to have their daughter's belongings packed away.

I hope that's what they did, anyway, she thought, crossing her fingers. *They might just as easily have bundled everything up and donated it to the Salvation Army. In that case, we're out of luck.*

Glancing up at the high ceiling overhead, she reminded herself that the attic was on her list of things to cope with, anyway. Everything there would need to be inventoried, just like the contents of the rest of the mansion, before she could even consider putting the house up for sale.

"Do I have my work cut out for me!" she said aloud.

Lindsay found it easier to concentrate on the tasks ahead of her than to come to terms with the fact that she didn't really want to sell the house. After spending a night under her own roof, she was more reluctant than ever to part with the home that had sheltered her family for an entire century.

But whenever the notion of staying strayed into her mind, the difficulties seemed overwhelming. She would have to work and work hard to support both herself and an aging house. Ferndale was village size, the attractive business establishments ranged along Main Street largely tourist-oriented. Eureka, seventeen miles to the north, was within easy commuting distance. But even in that bigger town could she find a clothing store in need of a manager? One that would start her off at even half of what she'd been making at Denim Ala Mode?

It would need to be at least that much, Lindsay estimated. Repairs and property taxes would cancel out savings on rent. And then, of course, there was the 'Vette.

She sighed as she glanced out at the porte cochere where her ancestors' horse and buggy had once stood. Unfortunately another eighteen months' worth of payments still remained to be made on the sleek white convertible. The Corvette was a dream car; she loved it! But once, in brutal honesty, she had admitted to her roommates that she'd bought it to make up to herself for all the other good things she was forced to miss out on because of her demanding job.

Now it looked as if the expensive automobile would have to compensate her for parting with this lovely old home too.

Resolutely Lindsay turned her back on the window. She rummaged in her purse for a pen and notebook. As long as she intended to hunt for Renae's possessions, she might just as well begin her inventory at the same time.

At the flip of a switch, electric light flooded the vast third story of the old Queen Anne mansion. But relief that she wouldn't be required to operate by candlelight turned to dismay as Lindsay caught sight of the attic's contents. Erik's quip about his family never throwing anything away now seemed less of a joke than a prediction. Here, her astonished gaze ranged over storage boxes and cartons by the hundreds. Luggage in all sizes and shapes. An astonishing variety of appliances and sporting goods: ponderous ice chests, tents, wringer washing machines, skis, and a bicycle that looked as if it might have been constructed by the Wright Brothers ten years before they took to the air at Kitty Hawk.

There was furniture too. And the baby things! Cribs and cradles, high chairs and prams. Not to mention an assortment of playthings numerous and varied enough to stock a long-ago branch of Toys Я Us.

Dizzily Lindsay set down her pen and paper. The objects in the attic alone would fill a dozen notebooks. Some of these things might be valuable. Others were undoubtedly junk. It would take expertise to sort them out. Expertise and time.

"Like a couple of years!" she groaned.

But Lindsay had tackled hard jobs before. Sooner or later it could be managed, she knew. The trick was to set priorities. Right at the top of the list was keeping her promise to Erik.

After some thought she decided that the luggage was the logical place to start in her search for Renae's possessions. That still left a multitude of choices. Along with suitcases, hatboxes, and Gladstone bags, at least twenty-five or thirty huge steamer trunks testified to the da Silva family's love of travel. Each piece of luggage had a key taped to its top and was festooned with bright tags: Cunard White Star Line, Wagon-Lits Cooks, Simplon-Orient Express, P&O Line.

Boy, had the da Silvas traveled, Lindsay marveled. And they hadn't traveled light, either!

Unlocking a brassbound trunk at random, she caught a lingering whiff of camphor as she removed first a heavy piece of oiled paper, then a cotton sheet that had been tucked around the top of the trunk to keep out dust. One at a time she lifted out the garments inside, holding them high to avoid any contact with the floor.

"Wow!" she breathed in awe. "These things ought to be in a museum!"

Everything in that particular trunk had obviously been handmade in the Orient. Probably, Lindsay thought, they dated from some trip Luzia and Bartolomew had taken to the Far East before World War I. Multicolored embroidery on a lovely silk shawl told a charming story of life in a Chinese village. Deeply knotted fringe edged the hem of the wrap, adding to its bygone elegance.

She found herself smiling as next she lifted out a man's shirt. But what a shirt! The garment was rich with color and design. A lady's blouse came next, made of purple silk, with white trim and a *ruyi* collar. Riverscapes were worked into the cloth in dainty gold stitches and Peking knot. At the bottom of the trunk lay a silk-brocade kimono. The creamy fabric was patterned with exotic birds, chrysanthemums, and fans.

Lindsay didn't even want to think of the painstaking hours it must have required to fashion each of those exquisitely embroidered designs. She knew that such a time-consuming craft was a relic of the past.

Reluctantly she returned these end-of-an-era treasures to the trunk. Spying a Lane cedar chest in with the suitcases, she opened it and unearthed clothes her own mother had worn as a young adult. A high-school yearbook nestled among prom dresses. Swimsuits straight from an Esther Williams movie were intertwined with a "mod" collection of miniskirts by Mary Quant. One of them was folded around a Beatles album.

Lindsay blinked back tears at the sight of her mother's cherished belongings. Flipping through the yearbook, she caught her breath at the sight of a certain photo. The face smiling out at her had high-winged brows, luminous brown eyes, delicate features, and a stubborn chin marked by a shallow cleft. Clouds of black hair sprang from a deep widow's peak. It could have been a photo of herself she was looking at, but the girl in the old yearbook had been named Mercedes da Silva.

The close family resemblance among

different generations of her kin jogged Lindsay's memory as to why she had come to the attic in the first place. If she kept on letting nostalgia overcome her, she would never find Renae's things!

Industriously she set to work, sorting through men's nautical wear, women's fripperies, lacy infants' christening gowns, Victorian "whites," yellowed linens. By midafternoon hunger drove her downstairs for a sandwich. Still holding it when she returned to the attic, she stood in the doorway, pensively chewing the last few bites while appraising the stacks of luggage remaining to be searched.

From that vantage point she spotted a pair of matching trunks that had escaped her notice earlier. Powdered with dust, they had been shoved into a far corner. Straining with the effort, Lindsay tugged first one, then the other out to where the light was better. She held her breath as the key clicked rustily in the lock.

The moment the lid creaked open, she knew she had found what she'd been seeking. The discovery made her gasp. She had forgotten how wealthy the da Silva family was before the stock market crash of 1929. Now she reminded herself of Helga Jensen's recollections, how sixty years later she had told Erik about Renae returning from Europe with trunks filled with extravagant clothes.

That description hardly did them justice, she thought. What she was looking at was *haute couture* — one-of-a-kind designer originals from the top fashion houses in the world of that between-wars era.

Lindsay wiped suddenly damp palms on the tails of her denim shirt. If she'd had a pair of surgical gloves to wear while handling these treasures, she would have slipped them on. The dresses were almost too precious to touch. Taking a deep breath, she carefully lifted out a swingy dance dress. Hundreds of hand-sewn jet beads rippled across the bodice as the garment swayed into the air. Layers of fringe tangoed from side to side.

"I can just picture someone doing the Charleston in this," she murmured. "Some 'It Girl.' It's definitely the cat's pajamas!"

The silly bit of twenties' slang made her smile and eased the tension. She continued to handle the dress with the utmost respect, however. Clothing was Lindsay's business. Her current job required that she feature the trendiest styles of the '90s in her shops, but college courses in the history of costume had given her a thorough knowledge of fashion throughout the ages. Even before spotting the designer's label stitched into a seam, she'd known that this garment was something very special indeed.

Jeanne Lanvin, the designer, had been a legend in her own time.

So, like Coco Chanel and Madeleine Vionnet — the twenties' "architect among dressmakers" — had Poiret been. The next garment Lindsay lifted out of the trunk was an exquisite short-sleeved evening gown created by this French designer. In awe she studied the contrasts in texture and color that made the dress such a knockout. Its maker had matched a gold lamé bodice with a plum velvet skirt, then merged the fabrics into a gilt belt that was a clever confection of soft and metallic threads. The puffy hem was unusual, too, hanging as it did in irregular lengths.

Very carefully Lindsay replaced the gown in its muslin wrappings. Lying beneath it in the trunk was a long box. Across the paper label strutted the designer's name: Mariano Fortuny. Her hands trembled as she lifted the box out of the niche where it had lain for so many decades.

Raising the lid, she realized that she had found something extremely rare. The peplos-style gown was made of creamy white silk. Cut in points, the overblouse shimmered with pin-striped, clear glass beads. The skirt swayed at a touch, dancing in her hands.

It came clear of the box to reveal a second garment by the same maker lying in a deceptively careless-looking bundle. Lindsay recalled that dresses such as these were always stored flat, never hung, because the weight of the beads and other ornamentation would put too great a strain on the fabric. As in this turquoise dress, Fortuny had created a secret method of creasing fabric into a shimmering maze of pleats never duplicated by any other couturier.

It seemed mind-boggling that a girl from a small town would have possessed such a fabulous wardrobe. Lindsay guessed that the expensive clothing, which was accompanied by every imaginable accessory, must have been a not-so-subtle bribe by Renae's parents to coax her into changing her mind. They must have hoped that by wearing such lovely things while mingling with the international set, Renae would forget all about the unsuitable young man back home in Ferndale.

But it hadn't worked, Lindsay reflected.

Renae had rejected her wealthy suitor's proposal, insisting that the love she felt for Nils Thorvaldsen was powerful enough to last for all time.

A trifle enviously, Lindsay wondered if she would ever have a love of her own that great. Probably not, she concluded. After all, by the age of twenty-six, one must be well past the age for a grand passion.

Still. . . .

Starting to unpack the second trunk, she wondered whether Erik Thorvaldsen was seeing any girl seriously. Then she laughed at the notion. They had teamed up to *end* the feud, not add fire to it!

Twenty minutes later she sat back on her heels in disgust. The trunk had been stuffed with everything from chemises to fur-trimmed coats and Art Deco earrings. But it hadn't contained a single scrap of paper.

That doesn't make sense, she thought. *Nils* must *have written to Renae. For a few months, at least. That's the only explanation for the turnaround in her behavior after her twenty-first birthday.*

Then it dawned on her that this wasn't necessarily true. There could have been another reason for the absence of correspondence in the trunk.

If Nils jilted Renae, she might have torn up all his letters in a rage!

But in that case, why would she have spent day after day out in the gazebo, waiting for him to return?

"Who knows!"

Exasperated, Lindsay repacked the trunk. Then, loathe to give up, she rummaged through the last dozen pieces of luggage in the attic. Finally she realized that outside night had long since fallen and that she was tired enough to fall asleep right there on the dusty floor.

Erik is going to be so disappointed! she thought.

Stumbling back downstairs, she admitted that it was for his sake she had put so much effort into the search. Knowing how much he cared for his family, she had wanted to help him.

His family, the last of the da Silvas reminded herself pointedly. *The Thorvaldsens!*

Chapter Five

Lindsay had a dreadful time falling asleep that night. Not that she wasn't tired. Physically she felt downright exhausted. All the lifting, bending, tugging, and stretching had given her muscles an unaccustomed workout. But the thoughts stomping through her head made relaxation almost impossible.

Oddly enough, the story of their ancestors that Erik had shared with her hadn't kept her awake for a minute the night before. Not even his assertion that he had *seen* Renae. Crediting that claim required a stretch of the imagination. Yet it didn't seem beyond the realm of possibility. In some of the countries where Lindsay had grown up, her *amahs* — nursemaids — had passed on many unorthodox superstitions in the folklore they used as bedtime stories. Erik's tale wasn't as strange as some of the other things she'd heard and half believed as a child.

She gave a dejected sigh. If only she could have found those letters! Or Renae's diary with an address jotted in it. Even an old advertisement, placed by a master furniture craftsman in search of a talented apprentice. Any of those things could have provided the starting point in their efforts to learn what had happened to Nils Thorvaldsen.

Could have been the first step in ending the feud between her family and Erik's.

Common sense told Lindsay she wouldn't be around to learn the end of the story no matter how it turned out. She'd be back in the city, busy with her career. The new owners would be living in her family's old house. The da Silvas and the Thorvaldsens would never need to worry about each other again, whether or not the feud was ever settled.

Too bad she couldn't have her cake and eat it too, Lindsay thought discontentedly. Too big or not, this was a wonderful house. She would like to stay right here and live in it. Its sale would bring a steep price, though. She would never need to worry about money for car payments or anything else again. Unless she decided *not* to sell. Then she'd have her hands full, trying to support a Butterfat mansion as well as herself.

If she managed to do that, could she

achieve a peaceful coexistence with the Thorvaldsen family? One member, in particular?

Lindsay smiled into the darkness as she pictured the owner of Classic Restorations. Next time they had dinner together, they might even manage to taste what they were eating. Beginning to relax, she tugged the downy comforter higher. If they had a second dinner at Filini's North, would Marta be wearing another antique gown?

Remembering the racks of look-alike jeans and jackets at Denim Ala Mode, she thought that Erik's cousin had been pretty astute in describing modern-day clothing as turned out with cookie cutters. Such a description certainly didn't fit the garments she'd spent all day rummaging through up in the attic. The things once worn by her ancestors were unique.

Probably worth a great deal too, Lindsay reflected thoughtfully. As well as being in demand. Look at the way the customers in Filini's North had ogled that turn-of-the-century outfit Marta had been wearing.

All day long a wild possibility had been tiptoeing around in her head. Now it elbowed its way to the surface.

"What if I were to sell the clothing instead of the house?" she said, testing the notion on the darkness. "Recycle those vintage fashions right back into the 1990s?"

She couldn't do that and keep her present job at the same time, of course. Working for Denim Ala Mode barely left her a moment to breathe. And she was tired of it. It wasn't just the time constraints that were beginning to pall. She was also fed up to the point of boredom with the sameness of the clothes her shops featured, and of the customers who bought them. They were practically clones of one another. People on the cutting edge of success whose hairstyles, clothing styles, life-styles were endlessly duplicated, as if to leave no doubt in anyone's mind that they were on their way up.

Lindsay knew that if what was "in" changed overnight, the way it had when the "New Look" exploded on the fashion scene in 1947, or when the miniskirt hit the market in the middle of the mod, mod sixties, those same customers would abandon their upscale denims so fast it would make poor old Levi Strauss spin in his grave.

Something else had happened back in the sixties, she reminded herself. A lot of people started dressing to please themselves. Not only the beatniks and the hippies, but others, not so easily categorized, who were tired of following the fashionable herd. Over the last few decades the trend had grown.

Now in the nineties, the "retro" look was downright popular, Lindsay reflected. Vintage clothing was almost a fashion force. Not in the elegant downtown locations. But out in the neighborhoods, all sorts of funky little shops were providing an interesting alternative to the monotony of the malls.

"I wonder how it would feel to be my own boss?" she asked aloud.

A couple of days earlier she had felt a twinge of envy at Erik's freedom to do the sort of work he loved at his own pace. Like him, Marta and Tony had detoured out of the fast lane, giving up promising careers to open their restaurant. That hadn't been accomplished by wishful thinking. All three of them had taken positive action and plenty of risks. Climbed out on a shaky limb to prove they were equal to the challenge.

While she longed to do the same, it was hard to ignore the scary fact that nine out of ten new businesses folded up within a year of the time they were launched. If she failed, she could lose everything. Including this wonderful mansion that had been in her family for a hundred years.

But by risking everything she had a chance to keep it.

Right at first it wouldn't be necessary to earn a whole lot, she told herself persuasively. *Just enough to keep myself and the house afloat.*

She awoke the next morning with a dozen new ideas in mind. *There's enough stuff in the attic to stock a vintage-clothing shop a dozen times over,* she mused. *I can add more eventually by going to yard sales and auctions. Maybe buying other old trunks that have been in storage for generations. There must be plenty of families like Erik's and mine, who don't discard things just because they've seen a little use.*

The thought of Erik strengthened her resolve still further. What a Thorvaldsen could do, a da Silva could certainly accomplish. Better!

She began setting priorities. *First thing to do is decide where to set up shop. I'll also need to get pricing guides and every reference book on antique clothing I can lay my hands on. Find out exactly what I have, where it came from and when, and what it's worth in today's*

108

market. Then figure out ways to display those fabulous clothes to their best advantage.

Not until the 1920s, she knew, had couturiers realized the value of having live models show off their eye-catching apparel. In the 1800s, "pattern cards" were used, flat sketches that gave a general idea of how a garment was to look. By the turn of the century, "fashion dolls" were being sent across the Atlantic to demonstrate the designs created by legendary Parisian dressmakers, such as Worth. Then full-sized store dummies were used. But nothing added panache to a garment the way a real, live mannequin could.

Lindsay resolved to show off her stock by modeling clothes from different eras as she waited on customers. Marta would make an attractive walking advertisement too. Maybe they could make a trade: the loan of a wardrobe of lovely old dresses in exchange for word-of-mouth advertising and a discreet placard at Filini's North promoting Lindsay's shop.

But all those details could be worked out after she found a location. She hadn't noticed a single empty store in Ferndale. However, Eureka might be preferable, anyway. The larger city had a well-known historic district that attracted tourists year round. With luck she could find a space to rent there in Old Town.

Hopping out of bed, Lindsay hastily smoothed back the covers. There wasn't a minute to waste if she intended to go into business for herself!

Perched comfortably on a high ladder, Erik Thorvaldsen caulked the seam of a downspout. The throb of a powerful car engine caused him to turn and stare into the next yard. He caught a quick glimpse of an all-too-familiar-looking woman backing down the driveway in a sleek white convertible. The Corvette kicked up a meteor shower of gravel, then zoomed down the street in a spurt of high-octane power.

Bet she watches Shirley Muldowney on ESPN! he thought.

Thoughts of the famous female drag racer and Erik's grin both faded as he wondered where Lindsay could be headed in such an almighty hurry. She wouldn't be going back to the city already, would she? What about putting the house up for sale?

"Never mind that," he growled aloud as his conscience gave him a nudge. "What about those letters?"

Not that he would have admitted it, but

thoughts of Lindsay Dorsett had been pestering Erik for the past thirty-six hours. Yesterday he'd kept putting up his hammer and turning around, certain that at any moment she would appear on her side of the fence and call across to him. He'd imagined her waving an old letter, smiling that dynamite smile while she read off the return address to him. But though he'd worked an hour past his usual quitting time last night, Lindsay had never so much as stuck her head out the door.

Now this morning she'd gone speeding off. Without so much as a glance in his direction.

That rankled. Not that he *cared*, of course. They weren't exactly destined to be pals. For a few minutes the other night, though, he'd come close to forgetting who she was. Who he was. When he'd gazed into those gorgeous brown eyes of hers there in the restaurant, it had felt almost as if they were two lost souls who'd been reunited after a long, long separation.

Ridiculous, he grumbled silently now, letting his imagination run wild like that. Lindsay wasn't Renae, and he wasn't Nils. They might resemble their ancestors in appearance, but that was all. They were completely different from the couple who had

111

loved and lost two generations ago. Worlds apart. Why, they didn't share a single interest!

She was a city girl. A world traveler. He was happy right here in the small town where he'd been born.

Lindsay drove a fancy Corvette. He got around in a beat-up old Chevy truck.

She was a da Silva. He was a Thorvaldsen.

The only thing they had in common was an old tragedy that had brought sorrow and resentment to both their families.

Clenching his strong, firm jaw, Erik turned back to the task at hand.

Lindsay slowed down to speed limit while trundling across the picturesque, Roman-style bridge spanning the Eel River. But the instant she turned onto the freeway, she let the 'Vette out, racing northward up 101 with a feeling of eager anticipation.

Soon after entering Eureka, she passed a sizable shopping mall. Not what she wanted, Lindsay thought, looking ahead as signs pointed the way to Old Town. The historic section comprised a several-blocks stretch of nineteenth-century buildings angled along the scenic waterfront. Even this early in the day, parking spaces were at a premium. Spying a car pulling out near the corner of Second and M Streets, she quickly took advantage of the opening. It wasn't until she set the brake that she realized the manicured grounds across the street were not park, but rather extensive landscaping surrounding the most astonishing building she had ever clapped eyes on.

A sign behind the spiky, wrought-iron fence stated that the Carson Mansion had been built for a lumber baron in the 1880s. The main tower of the elaborate Victorian structure rose to a fifth story — no, sixth, Lindsay saw in bemusement, while numerous highly embellished turrets and gables soared upward from the three main floors of the imposing home. Nowadays the mansion was the property of a private men's club. Just as well it wasn't open to the public, she decided. Otherwise she would no doubt have spent all day there, poking into every fascinating corner.

Turning away from the famous landmark, Lindsay made her way into the heart of Old Town. Here, along with the historic buildings, many elegant touches of yesteryear had been retained. Sauntering across a brick crosswalk, she smiled at the sight of iron benches placed invitingly wherever sidewalk space permitted. Planters bright with spring blooms and colorful hanging flower baskets decorated many of the bakeries, cafes, and galleries she passed.

On a side street she spotted a vintage clothing shop. Good news and bad news, she thought, noting that it didn't open until noon. Competition — but also proof positive that a good market for antique garments existed in the area.

Strolling on, Lindsay enjoyed the north coast ambience as she window-shopped. But the farther she walked, the less hopeful she became about the possibility of finding a space here in Old Town at a moderate rental cost. Other would-be shop owners would be vying for any likely opening.

The truth of this suspicion was underscored by the sign in the window of an antique shop. *Lost Our Lease*, it declared.

The shop was located on the ground floor of a tall, narrow Victorian house built in the Eastlake Stick style. It was a charming building — or would have been, had the façade been properly maintained. But paint was flaking, oak and walnut trim looked shabby, and the incised decorations needed a thorough cleaning to restore their sharp appeal.

She stepped inside, thinking that perhaps the shop owner might be induced to fill her in on the potential for renting a commercial space in Old Town. The place was called Beautiful Dreamer. As Lindsay entered, a music-box tinkle of that nostalgic old Stephen Foster air welcomed her. The proprietor, a little dumpling of a lady who appeared to be in her middle sixties, excused herself from another customer and bustled forward.

"Good morning," Lindsay replied to her greeting. "What a lot of nice things you have here!"

Leafy green plants in Victorian cachepots provided a restful change from crowded shelves bristling with Oriental porcelains and elegant cut-glass scent bottles. Lithographed sheet music was artfully arranged on a rosewood piano. But what drew her forward for a closer examination was the large assortment of old toys and games.

"I could offer you a very good price on some of these collectibles," the shop owner said. Lindsay noticed that she wore a floor-length skirt and a ruffled shirtwaist with leg-o'-mutton sleeves, very much in keeping with the atmosphere of a place whose merchandise averaged a hundred years old. "You may have seen the sign out front. After thirty-one years in the same location, my lease has run out. New owners have bought my building. I had thought I was to have the rest of the summer to relocate, but they told me yesterday that they will be able to have this place refurbished sooner than expected. I have only thirty days to find a new location."

"That doesn't give you much time," Lindsay commiserated. "Have you found someplace else to go yet?"

The proprietor, who introduced herself as Adelaide Whitecliff, shook her head. "No, and I've looked and looked. Nothing affordable is halfway suitable. The last few years many of the shop spaces have been taken over by professional people. This building will be turned into offices for a married couple who are both lawyers."

"I noticed quite a lot of doctors, dentists, and attorneys mixed in with the gift shops and cafés," Lindsay commented. "What bad luck for you!" Herself too, she thought in disappointment. If an experienced shop owner like Miss Whitecliff was having trouble relocating, what chance had she of finding a place to rent?

Glumly she studied the assortment of metal and wooden toys. On the drive up to

Eureka it had occurred to Lindsay that one means of raising start-up money for her new business would be to sell some of the items she had run across before starting her search of the attic trunks.

"Actually, I'm not here to buy today," she said frankly. "I ran across a collection of old board games in a house I recently inherited. One was called The Man in the Moon. The Visit of Santa Claus was another. I'm pretty sure a third game had something to do with Nellie Bly."

The older woman gave a knowledgeable nod. "That would be Round the World with Nellie Bly," she confirmed. "It was copyrighted by McLoughlin Bros. in 1901. You shouldn't have any trouble selling your games to collectors, provided they are in at least average condition. I'm only sorry I won't be able to handle them for you. But right now I'm at my wits' end, wondering what to do with the stock I already have on hand."

"It must be hard to think of moving when you're so well established." Lindsay looked out at the bustling street. "I imagine you've seen all sorts of changes during the years you've been here."

"Dear me, yes. This part of town wasn't the least bit fashionable when I first rented the store," Miss Whitecliff reminisced. "In fact, back in the 1960s there was a movement afoot to tear down the whole neighborhood. Some of the city fathers wanted to replace Two Street — Second Street, strangers call it — with one of those elevated freeways. That way, they figured they could keep the new part of town separate from the waterfront."

"Well, Addie, you have to admit it was a pretty disreputable area," the woman customer chimed in with a chuckle. "Long on saloons and dance halls, and short on artsy-craftsy shops in those days! The fine old houses along First, Two, and Third Streets had gotten pretty seedy looking after standing around in the salt air for eighty or ninety years. Even the Carson mansion was an eyesore."

"You certainly couldn't say that now," Lindsay remarked. "What happened to save the historic district?"

"Folks all over the state got together and launched a project called Century III," Addie told her. "First they voted down the freeway idea. Then they coaxed the Federal government into making some low-cost loans so they could start sprucing up the old sector. A lot of hard work went into making the waterfront a credit to the town, 'stead of a blight."

"Their efforts really paid off."

"Yes, but now the neighborhood's grown so popular that I'm being evicted," Addie complained. "I've built up a mighty faithful clientele. I know my customers would trail along if I set up shop in another part of town or moved a few miles north to Arcata. But antiques need a special setting. So far, I haven't had the heart to settle for some flimsy modern building that would do just as well for a tire outlet or video-rental store."

An idea was nudging Lindsay. Before it had a chance to develop, the opening notes of "Beautiful Dreamer" resounded through the shop again. A couple dressed in business suits breezed in. The woman whipped out a tape measure. "Reception area," Lindsay heard the man say, gesturing while his wife marked down feet and inches in a notebook. "Should work fine if we keep the furniture small scale. But that leaves one or the other of us with a windowless office. It'll be like the Black Hole of Calcutta in there."

"Not if we let Erik follow through on his skylight idea."

Having deduced that these were the building's new owners, Lindsay had only half listened to their plans. Now the name Erik snagged her attention. She turned to exclaim in surprise, "Erik Thorvaldsen of Classic Restorations in Ferndale?"

"Why, yes." The redheaded woman reeled in her tape measure, excitement glowing in her animated face. "Do you know him?"

"I do, as a matter of fact," Lindsay claimed. "Right now he's hard at work refurbishing the Butterfat mansion next to mine."

"He does absolutely marvelous work, doesn't he? I'm Eva Simms," the woman added, holding out her hand.

Lindsay clasped it, introducing herself in turn. "Miss Whitecliff was telling me that this building is to be turned into law offices. That sounds like a major undertaking."

"It certainly is," Eva Simms agreed. "We're still recovering from the shock of having Erik change his mind about being able to do the work for us this summer. We thought sure we'd have to wait months, maybe even years to be able to afford a Classic Restorations job, didn't we, Clayton? But just the other night he called —"

Her husband looked pointedly at his watch. "Honey, have you forgotten our

120

lunch appointment? We're supposed to meet Marv at Lazio's in three minutes."

"Ohmigosh, the CPA! Gotta run," the woman called back over her shoulder as she hastened toward the door. "Give Erik our regards."

"I must say they *seem* pleasant enough, even though they *are* evicting you," the woman customer remarked, coming forward to set a mechanical, cast-iron gadget on the sales counter. "Wrap up this Jonah and the Whale bank for me, will you, Addie? It'll make a nice addition to my collection."

A nice expensive addition, Lindsay thought, somewhat awed when the four-hundred-dollar purchase price was rung up. She hadn't dreamed old toys were so valuable!

"Thank you, Mrs. Butler." Addie tucked away the customer's check. "I've been keeping an eye out for that Leap Frog bank you asked me to find for you. But right now everything's at sixes and sevens."

"Just be sure not to move without letting me know your new address." Mrs. Butler tucked the box under her arm as carefully as if it contained a fragile and very precious piece of jewelry. "Even if you have to go clear to Crescent City to find a new place, I'll stick with you. It's worth driving a few extra miles to do business with a dealer I like and trust."

This vote of confidence brought tears to Addie's eyes. Other customers had told her the same thing. But it was clear to Lindsay that the problem of finding a suitable new location was weighing heavily on her mind.

Though there hadn't been time to mull the idea over thoroughly, she gave way to impulse. "Addle, how would you feel about relocating to Ferndale?"

"Like someone had just handed me Ali Baba's lamp and told me to give it a good rub," Addie promptly retorted. "Matter of fact, I drove down there just the other day. Those fancy shops along Main Street never seem to lack for tenants, worse luck. There's a waiting list a yard long for any space that becomes available."

"That's good news because it means the village attracts plenty of tourist business," Lindsay said, looking on the bright side. "Someone I know recently opened a restaurant in one of the beautiful old Butterfat mansions there. That being the case, I see no reason why the family home I just inherited couldn't do double duty as part commercial space and part residential too. There are several large ground-floor rooms that flow right into one another on both sides of the central entry hall. If most of the furnishings were moved to other parts of the house, the space would be ideal for two good-sized shops."

While Addie was catching her breath, Lindsay explained her interest in establishing a vintage-clothing business. "I set out this morning to hunt for a location here in Old Town. Now I realize that's unfeasible, especially since I'm starting out on a shoe-string. But if there's a way to attract customers, having my home and shop under the same roof would be an ideal arrangement. That's where you come in, Addie. Your clientele is already built up. If they're willing to follow. . . ."

Addie tucked away her handkerchief. "Antiquers are a loyal bunch. Especially when a dealer has worked as hard as I have to fill in the gaps in their collections. I can't think of anyplace that would make a better showcase for lovely old things than a Butterfat mansion. People would fall all over themselves to come on down to a location like that."

There had never been space enough to carry vintage clothing in her own store, Addie added. "It's a specialty and one that's begun to become extremely popular.

With decent merchandise and an attractive location, you ought to do right well."

The merchandise was more than decent, Lindsay knew. But Ferndale, after all, was just a village. Was the location attractive enough to pull in new customers as well as Beautiful Dreamer's faithful old crowd?

Now that push came to shove, she was starting to get cold feet. She loved challenges, but it would be two livelihoods, hers and Addie's both, that she would be risking.

"Listen," she said with a gulp, "I'm not totally committed to this plan yet. Can you give me a week? Once I do make up my mind, there'll be zoning permits to see about, insurance to arrange — dozens of details, in fact."

"You'll also need to check my references," Addie reminded her in a no-nonsense tone. She scribbled a name and number on the back of one of her business cards. "I'll call my banker right away and give him instructions to answer your questions. Naturally, these things work both ways. I would need to see the house you were telling me about before I made any firm arrangements."

They agreed to give each other a week's grace. By the following Thursday each of them pledged to have a firm decision ready.

Lindsay was simmering with excitement as she left the antique shop for the return drive. Fastening her seat belt, she gave the 'Vette its head as she guided the white convertible down the freeway. Self-doubts weren't a large part of her makeup, and usually decisions came easily to her. But her whole future was riding on what she chose to do in the next week. She didn't dare blunder.

Dodging a couple of the worst chuckholes, she pulled into her own driveway. As she climbed out, she spotted the ladder propped up against the house next door and felt a twinge of guilt. Erik must be wondering why she hadn't let him know the results of her search. She really needed to get over there and give him the bad news before concentrating exclusively on her own concerns.

As it turned out, that wasn't necessary. Erik had been keeping an eye out for her. Less than a minute later she saw him round the corner and turn in at her front gate.

"Hello, Erik." The wary look flickering in his eyes advertised his mistrust of anyone related by blood to the da Silvas.

Lindsay had been aiming at dredging up a friendly smile for him until she saw the tilt of his jaw and the way his blond brows were pulled together in a scowl. Friendly wasn't ever going to be part of their mutual experiences, she warned herself.

"Hello." Erik was ashamed of his growling reply as soon as it emerged. He hadn't come over here to jump down her throat. Just to collect a bit of information. But with every step closer he drew to Lindsay, the more confused he felt. He kept losing sight of the fact that, by tradition, she was the enemy.

Lindsay hadn't missed his gruff tone. If they didn't watch out, they'd be screaming at each other, like Olin and Felice in the post office.

"I'd have been on my way over to see you in about another two minutes," she assured him, hating the defensive way she sounded. As if she hadn't expected him to believe her. Even though they were Thorvaldsen and da Silva, he *had* asked for her help. That ought to count for something!

She looked angry. Regretful too. With this insight, Erik stumbled onto the truth. Lindsay hadn't found the letters, he realized. Because of that she'd been dreading this encounter.

Disappointment hit him in a wave. He'd allowed himself to get too hopeful. Olin was as dear to him as any grandfather could be, and he had wanted so much to give the old man the gift of an easy mind to ease him through his last few years.

But his dream seemed destined never to come true.

Glancing back as she unlocked the front door, Lindsay felt her breath catch. How dejected Erik looked! As though he had already guessed what she needed to tell him!

Last night in the restaurant he had reached out to her, offering moral support while he told that sad story of their ancestors. Now, without thinking twice, Lindsay extended her hand and returned the favor. In silent encouragement she curled her fingers around his strong, bronzed arm and squeezed.

"Take heart," the gesture seemed to imply. Oddly enough, it did make Erik feel better.

Lindsay was a kindhearted person, but she wasn't usually given to such impulsiveness. Especially with strangers. The trouble was, she told herself as she broke the touch and pushed on into the entry hall, Erik didn't seem like a stranger at all. At times she could have sworn they'd been best friends for years.

"No luck," she blurted out the bad news as soon as he'd followed her inside. "Believe it or not, I searched for more than ten hours yesterday without finding so much as a scribble among Renae's things."

Erik knew she had only agreed to look for the letters as a favor to him. They didn't mean a thing to her. Yet now she was apologizing and as downcast as if it were her own favorite relative who was pushing ninety with one heart attack already under his belt.

Unable to resist touching her, he reached up and brushed a cloud of dark hair back from her forehead. Gazing into her warm brown eyes, a mist of *déjà vu* spun in his head. That look — just for him. When and where had he seen it before?

"Of course I believe you," he assured her. "Don't take it so hard, Lin. This is just a temporary setback. Something's bound to —"

Intent on his words, Lindsay hardly heard the phone jangle. No one had ever called her Lin before. On his lips, the nickname sounded exactly right.

Before she could tell him so, the strident summons pealed again. This time it forced

128

its way into her consciousness. "Hold on," she murmured, taking a reluctant step toward the parlor and the shrilling telephone. "I'll be right back."

Erik's thoughts brooded with foreboding. While he made no effort to eavesdrop on the conversation in the next room, the rhythm of Lindsay's voice acted like a warning bell on his senses. Her sentences were short, her tone crisp and businesslike. She seemed almost to be speaking a different language from the one they had been using together.

Lindsay stepped from rug to tile, her pace reluctant, her eyes fixed on Erik's face. Just moments ago they'd been communicating on a friend-to-friend level, almost without words. Now his jaw was stony, his stance stiff, his thoughts locked inside.

He knew.

She told him, anyway.

"I'm sorry I won't be able to take a second stab at finding the letters," she murmured. "That was my boss on the phone, the president of Denim Ala Mode. He's — I'm afraid he's made me an offer I can't refuse."

Chapter Six

During the next few days Erik mentally apologized to Renae at least half a dozen times. There'd been moments in the past when he had felt impatient with her for just drooping around the gazebo until she caught pneumonia instead of pulling herself together and getting on with her life.

Now he understood just how she'd felt.

Even after telling himself there wasn't a chance in a thousand of Lindsay coming back, he had kept on hoping. He managed to find one unnecessary chore after another at the Jensens', while keeping an eye on the house next door. But it had been six days now since she'd left, speeding south as fast as the steel-belted radials on that fancy car of hers could spin. He'd almost run out of excuses to stick around, but he wasn't scheduled to start his new project until Monday. Until then —

The scrunch of wheels on gravel caused Erik to swing around so fast, he nearly took another header off the ladder. That slapdash approach reminded him of Lindsay's dragster-driving technique. Disappointment so real he could taste it hit him when he saw that the vehicle that had spurted into the next driveway was an undistinguished forest green van rather than a racy white Corvette.

The real estate agent, he concluded gloomily, come to post a For Sale sign on the gate. Realtors didn't usually drive around in five-year-old Plymouth Voyagers. But who else would have driven right up and made themselves at home on da Silva property?

The driver's door sprang open. A black-haired young woman leaped out of the van, stumbling a bit as though she were accustomed to exiting from a more low-slung chariot. Not even the potholed driveway slowed her down for long, however. From his high perch Erik watched while Lindsay flung her arms wide in an exuberant gesture.

It looked almost as if she were giving the house a hug. Erik felt a sappy inclination to snatch his handkerchief out of his back pocket and give his nose a firm blow. He was still tamping down the unexpected rush of emotion when the woman next door wheeled toward the fence, calling his name.

"Erik! Erik, are you over there? Erik, I'm back!"

From the moment he'd first laid eyes on Lindsay, Erik had felt a crackling rapport between them that was almost electric in intensity. Now the excitement in her voice gave him reason to believe that she might have felt some of the same attraction. By the time she stretched on tiptoe to peer over the fence, he had scrambled down from the ladder.

"Stay right there, Lin!" he shouted to her. "I'm on my way!"

He sprinted through the Jensens' back orchard, scrambled down the creek bank, sloshing as his momentum carried him farther than expected, then splashed up again on the other side of the fence. Apple blossoms scattered as he collided with a tree limb. He ricocheted back, then ducked underneath it to dart toward the woman who waited for him, laughing. Once more, her arms were stretched wide.

Erik folded her against his chest. Feeling his heartbeat echo hers, he wondered whether the same thoughts were going through her mind. Thoughts about belonging. About second chances.

"This is fantastic!" Scarcely able to believe his luck, he shook his head. "Just a couple of minutes ago I had myself convinced that I'd never see you again."

Lindsay was practically fizzing over with delight. Ten days earlier she had marched up the front walk of her family's old Butterfat mansion and felt a keen sensation of homecoming. Now Erik's enthusiastic welcome reprised that wonderful perception. His hug made her feel as if she had truly come home to stay.

"Oh, Erik, they offered me the most stupendous job!" Her words tripped over each other in their eagerness to tell him every single thing that had happened during her absence. "The board at Denim Ala Mode decided to expand their chain and open shops in every major mall in the West. They wanted *me* to be in charge of the California group. My boss said they'd been keeping an eye on my management techniques for years, grooming me for this position. I turned down a salary that would have made a lot of CEOs green with envy!"

Erik held her out at arm's length, feeling a surge of exuberance but telling himself his ears must have deceived him. "Turned down?"

"Yes!" Lindsay danced backward, unable to keep still. "After two days of nonstop meetings, I finally caught my breath and reminded myself this was the sort of schedule I'd be keeping the rest of my life if I didn't jump off the roller coaster right then and there. Sure, my career was skyrocketing! But where did that leave *me?*"

"A long way from home."

"That's exactly right!" Erik's reply had sounded awfully solemn. Lindsay wished he would smile again. His whole being seemed to light up when he did; she loved watching it happen. But now she grew earnest too. "This *is* my home, Erik. I intend to do my level best to stay here. Thanks to the inspiring example set by you and Marta and Tony —"

"You're going to try being your own boss?" His lean, paint-stained fingers wrapped around hers, congratulating her on the decision. "That's terrific. When do you start?"

"Arrangements are already underway." Lindsay explained that while she was tying up loose ends in the city, she had checked out Ferndale's zoning regulations by phone and applied for all the necessary licenses and permits to allow her to conduct business from her own home. "Then I asked Aunt Felice's executor to show Adelaide Whitecliff around the lower floor of my house."

"Who?" Keeping up with her was like trying to outdistance chain lightning, Erik decided.

Spinning toward the stately mansion, Lindsay motioned for him to come along. "Adelaide Whitecliff," she repeated. "Addle's owned an antique shop in Old Town Eureka for ages, but now her lease has run out, and she's going to rent space from me instead. You know her old building, Erik. It's that Eastman Stick Victorian you've been hired to remodel for Clayton and Eva Simms."

A brick-red glow flared across his cheeks. Talk about having an impulsive decision backfire!

"I don't get the connection," he growled.

Lindsay wondered why he was acting so defensive. He was free to accept any job he chose. It certainly wasn't *his* fault Addie had been evicted.

"Antiques are the connection except that I'm going to specialize in vintage clothing, so we won't be competing with each other. But Addie already has a well-established clientele. By sharing the premises with her, I'll get my business off to a much quicker start."

Erik quieted his conscience while listening to Lindsay's comments about what a helpful mentor Addie was sure to prove. By the time they reached her driveway, the focus of her chatter had veered to the million and one details she'd needed to cope with before leaving San Francisco.

"My roommates think I'm crazy, but they didn't have any trouble finding a third friend to split the apartment expenses with them," she said. "I put in a change of address, switched my checking and savings accounts to a Ferndale bank, and canceled several charge accounts. Then I decided that if I could learn to live without Visa, I could manage without the 'Vette too, so I traded it in."

Erik gaped in astonishment at the boxy green van in the driveway. "You swapped your beautiful sports car for *that?*"

"Yes, because it was the only way I could get out of debt." Lindsay sighed. "I loved the 'Vette. It was my Supergirl toy. But now all I want is to be my own woman. I can accomplish that a lot easier without a great big car payment hanging over my head for the next year and a half."

"Red ink never was my favorite color, either," he applauded the decision.

"Besides," Lindsay pointed out practically, "I plan on attending lots of yard sales and auctions in search of new stock. The van will earn its keep transporting all the bargains I find."

The last of the da Silvas was back in town to stay. This reflection worried Erik almost as much as it elated him.

By tacit agreement, they avoided discussing the feud. It was, however, on their minds.

Absolutely the first free minute she got, Lindsay promised herself, she would take another stab at finding those letters.

Positively the next visit he paid to his great-uncle Olin, Erik pledged, he would find a tactful way to mention that the old da Silva mansion would soon be doing double duty as commercial and residential property.

"Time seems to have sprouted wings!" Lindsay complained the Sunday after she had returned to Ferndale. "I still haven't brought down half the clothing from the attic for sorting and pricing. But you were right, Erik. It was important that I get in the habit of taking a few hours for myself every now and then. I wouldn't have missed this visit to the Avenue of the Giants for anything!"

He curved an arm around her shoulders, steadying her while she gazed up at the tops of the incredibly old and massive redwood trees that soared hundreds of feet above their heads.

"They're beautiful," he agreed. "So are you, Lin."

She straightened up in such surprise that she might have fallen had he not been there as a bulwark. "Oh, Erik, I enjoy your company so much," she murmured. "It bothers me to think that this might just be a case of opposites attracting."

That wasn't what made Erik uneasy. His disquiet arose from the fact that everything had been going along too smoothly. He couldn't shake the feeling that sooner or later their heritage was going to raise its troublesome head. But maybe if they just kept moving, it wouldn't catch up with them.

"Listen, Opposite," he sassed with a grin, "if you looked like me, I wouldn't *be* attracted. Want to go to an arts and crafts show over in Fortuna? I think the Rotary Club is putting on a barbecue later."

"That sounds like a lot of fun, but unfortunately I have a business appointment," Lindsay refused contritely. "Your cousin is coming over to try on some gowns."

Erik remembered the all-out effort it had taken to get his shoestring restoration business launched. Philosophically he guided Lindsay back to where they had left the truck.

Later that afternoon Lindsay stayed busy with needle and thread while Marta preened in the cheval mirror. "That's a terrible waste of time," Erik's cousin scolded. "Let me take that child's apron home with me. I can fix that torn ruffle in a jiffy on Mom's sewing machine."

"Thanks for the offer, but that wouldn't really be to my advantage." Holding up the little girl's pinafore she'd been mending, Lindsay explained that it had been sewn by hand ninety-odd years earlier. "Stitching a rip up on a machine would cut its value in half."

"Oops! Sorry. I didn't realize antique buyers were that finicky. Though I should have," Marta added. "That would be almost as bad as you bringing over a box of cake mix and offering to help Tony fill up the dessert cart!"

She had laid three elegant ensembles out across the bed. With a sigh of resignation, she eyed the long rows of tiny, cloth-covered buttons up the backs of each costume. "I've only just realized that zippers must not have come into regular use until midway through the 1930s," she commented. "Before that, it must have taken a full-time maid to get the family fastened together every morning."

"Along with another hardworking servant just to do the ironing." Back then, Lindsay said, petticoats and blouses were starched so heavily, they could stand up straight without anybody inside them.

A silver lining occurred to Marta as she fastened the collar of her shirtwaist with a lovely cameo pin. "Thanks to Gran's attic and the loan of these gowns from you, I've finally made friends with Tony's grandmother," she confided. "To her, modern styles are a disgrace. She tells me that in *her* day, no lady ever went shopping in San Francisco without her hat and gloves. That was before 1965. After the miniskirt came in, gracious living went to the dogs, according to her."

Lindsay wished that a mere change of clothing was all it would take to make the Thorvaldsen clan welcome her with open arms.

As if she had guessed what was in the other woman's thoughts, Marta swiveled around for a look at the floor-length taffeta skirt in the glass. Her glance kept right on traveling until it collided with Lindsay's.

"Am I the only one of Erik's relatives

you've met so far?"

She'd seen a lot of *him,* she thought defensively. In fact, they had been out several times since her return. Even on nights when they weren't dating, he almost always stopped by the house on his way home from work. It was the best part of her day.

"His parents and Gunnar's are still away on that cross-country trip," Lindsay hedged the main issue. "But tomorrow his brothers are coming to help him shift about a ton of furniture from the ground floor up to the attic so Addie and I can start setting up these big main rooms as showrooms." She gulped. "Their wives are coming along."

"Don't worry," Marta said easily. "You'll like them."

Lindsay admitted her secret fear. "I hope they like *me!*"

On the following day, three of the prettiest blondes Lindsay had ever seen showed up with their big, blond husbands. The women made no secret of their interest in the da Silva mansion and its contents. Chattering like magpies, they hauled knickknacks upstairs while their spouses helped Erik carry sofas, tables, escri- toires, and splat-back armchairs up to storage in the attic.

Leaving the men to shift all those cumbersome loads between floors, Erik's sisters-in-law followed Lindsay into one of the spare second-floor bedchambers for a look at the elaborate collection of accessories she had been assembling there.

"I couldn't imagine why anyone would want to run a secondhand shop until I saw this stuff," Ingrid said frankly. "But these things are absolutely unique. Look at the walking sticks, Shelby. Wouldn't Uncle Olin feel dapper, swaggering into church with one of them over his arm?"

"He'd love the spats too!" Karin gave Lindsay a friendly smile. "What are you going to call your vintage-clothing business?"

"Gladrags." Lindsay smiled back. "I'm hoping that the items I sell will make people feel good when they wear or collect them, so the name matches the philosophy of my shop."

She led the way into the adjacent room, where much of her flapper collection had been stored. "Nobody could sit around complaining in a dress like this," she said, holding up a drop-waisted chemise with a hem falling in diamond points to illustrate what she meant. "Doesn't it just make you want to get up and dance?"

"I see what you mean." Shelby, who was married to Erik's eldest brother, Knud, let out a crow of delight. "What a *wonderful* party dress!"

"Shelby, my love, you are five-ten and expecting twins," Ingrid teased her sister-in-law. "That dress was made for a petite young thing with a boyish figure."

"Which yours most definitely is not," Karin chimed in with a giggle.

"Count your blessings, Shelby. Boyish is out of style this week, anyway," Lindsay assured the expectant mother only half jokingly. Clothes were her business, and she really did know what was and was not in fashion on an almost daily basis. "But in the next room is something you might like to see. While unpacking a box the other day, I came across two of the most precious lace christening gowns any babies ever wore."

Shelby was enthralled with the tiny garments made of cobweb-fine lace and creamy satin. Without hesitation, Lindsay offered to lend them to her in a few months.

"I'd be honored to have your twins use them for their christening," she said with a smile. "Maybe having Thorvaldsen children wear heirlooms that have been cherished by several generations of da Silvas will help to heal the breech between our two families."

"Say, I've heard about some old scandal that nearly erupted into war between your family and Erik's," Karin remarked forthrightly. "What happened?"

Karin's Norwegian ancestors had emigrated to Canada, rather than to the United States. She and Dannel Thorvaldsen, both avid skiers, had met while on vacation in Calgary. Since they'd just been married a few months, she was only vaguely familiar with the family history.

Lindsay could have dodged the question, but she decided it was better to bring the old grievances out into the open. That way, at least, everyone would know the truth.

"Back in the 1920s my great-aunt and Erik's great-uncle fell in love," she said. "Nils and Renae were just teenagers, and their parents did everything possible to keep them apart. The love story had a tragic outcome: Nils left home and never returned, and Renae died not long afterward. The families blamed each other for the catastrophe and have been enemies ever since."

"All those years?"

Lindsay didn't blame Karin for sounding appalled. "Yes, nearly seven decades," she said, making it sound as ridiculous as it was. "I'm the last of the da Silvas. I didn't know anything about the feud until a few weeks ago, but I'm certainly ready to forgive and forget. Maybe you could encourage the rest of the Thorvaldsens to do the same thing."

"Well, of course!" Shelby promised, and Karin echoed the pledge.

Ingrid, however, didn't chime in until somebody nudged her. Then she gave her head a dubious shake. "Everyone else will come around, I'm sure," she agreed. "Everyone except Uncle Olin."

June first was targeted as the grand-opening date for Gladrags and the relocated Beautiful Dreamer. By the middle of May, Miss Whitecliff had transferred her entire stock of antiques to two of the downstairs "offices" in Lindsay's mansion. By removing the partition between the large parlor and formal dining room, they'd created more square footage for the shop than she'd had to work with at her Old Town location.

"What a luxury, being able to spread out a bit!"

Addie arranged a dowel-jointed Penny Wooden doll in the lap of a miniature Boston rocker adorned with red-rose decals. She plunked a topsy-turvy doll down on the table alongside the grouping. When Lindsay commented on the unusual toy, Addie flipped it upside down to display the second character head and body. It had been inspired by Harriet Beecher Stowe's firebrand book written before the Civil War, she said.

Next to it she made room for an 1890 Edison phonograph doll, newly acquired through a trade with another dealer. "This little beauty won't last long," she predicted complacently. "Some of my best customers are doll collectors."

Lindsay had been amazed to learn how many people were fascinated with old-time playthings. While Addie stocked impressive assortments of Depression glass, Wedgwood ceramics, sheet music, and other collectibles, toys were Beautiful Dreamer's specialty.

"A few weeks ago you mentioned having some games you'd be willing to sell," Addie reminded Lindsay. "Why don't you get them out and we'll take a look? You never know what might turn out to be valuable."

Her friend's tutelage and several reference books she had recently acquired had taught Lindsay that rarity, quality, and condition were the three main criteria used in determining an antique's worth. She retrieved the boxed games from the attic and gave them a good dusting. Then she presented them for Addie's appraisal. "I don't suppose this is one of those times when quality would be much of a factor," she said a trifle uncertainly.

"No, because the workmanship and design is identical on each of the sets issued under the same copyright," Addie agreed. "That makes the condition of the games all the more important."

She rated the Nellie Bly game as being in only average shape. No parts were missing, but several small, grubby handprints marred the surface of the board. The Man in the Moon game had obviously been some child's favorite. The box was tattered, as though it had been a constant rainy-day companion. The antique dealer pronounced the third game a real find, however. On careful examination, The Visit of Santa Claus, which dated from 1899, looked almost as new as if it had just been delivered by the reindeer that were part of the box's illustration.

"Lindsay, this is very fine. In mint condition," Addie declared. "A copy of this particular board game sold last year for seven hundred and twenty-five dollars, even though the corners of that box were foxed. I'd be surprised if yours didn't fetch eight hundred dollars."

The old game's current worth staggered Lindsay. "Wow! Oh, when I think of all the Monopoly and Scrabble sets we left behind in different embassies whenever we moved —"

"Take it easy. You didn't abandon any irreplaceable treasures," Addie assured her with a laugh. "Those games are so tremendously popular that the manufacturers produce millions of them every year. They'll never be collectors' items for the simple fact that there are far too many of them."

"I'm learning a lot about the law of supply and demand," Lindsay told Erik a few nights later as they made their way along the Woodley Island Marina. "There's a lot less vintage clothing than other types of antiques, because cloth was such a perishable necessity. Garments that weren't lost in fires or floods were usually handed down and worn until they were threadbare."

Fingers laced through hers, the tall young man in the dark suit cast an admiring glance at the floor-length dance dress she was wearing. It was made of rayon, once called "art silk." Long-sleeved and high-collared, its deep décolletage and draped side panel flattered her slender curves.

"I'm glad nobody added that gown to their collectibles until you'd had a chance to wear it this once, at least," he said frankly. "To tell the truth, I'm crazy about those ultrafeminine 'girl clothes' you dress up in every once in a while. What era is this one from?"

"The early 1940s," Lindsay answered, delighted that Erik had such an observant eye and that he wasn't too shy or blasé to express interest in women's clothes.

She loved dressing up in some of the lovely old costumes she'd found in the attic trunks. Almost as much fun was matching accessories and coiffures to the individual dresses. This evening she had swirled her long, dark hair into a pompadour. Wisely, however, suspecting that there might be an unusual amount of walking and climbing connected with tonight's activities, she decided not to wear the platform shoes with their extra-high heels that went along with this particular gown.

Following a number of other couples who were also dressed up for the occasion, they climbed the "ladder," a steep flight of narrow wooden steps that led up to the elevated dock. There, the H.M.S. *Bounty* had been berthed for this brief return visit to Humboldt Bay. Its sails were furled while in port, but the tall ship was an exact replica of the celebrated ship once commanded by Captain Bligh.

Erik had obtained tickets for a champagne reception aboard the old vessel. Delicious hors d'oeuvres and live music added a gala note to the festivities.

"Fond as I am of learning about the past, I'm glad I live now instead of then," Lindsay remarked as they came back out on deck sometime later. "Imagine, a whole crew being jammed into those cramped quarters for months or even years on those long voyages they took."

"It's just a lucky thing it was your people who were the sailors instead of mine," Erik agreed with a grin. "As much room as I take up, I'd have had a miserable time of it down there in that sweaty hold."

The mention of bygone generations had a dampening effect on what up until then had been a happy-go-lucky occasion. They fell silent on the drive back to Lindsay's house, each of them thinking about the ethnic differences that had kept their ancestors from understanding each other.

Lindsay wished she had never heard a word about their family histories. For weeks she had been falling more and more in love with Erik Thorvaldsen. How wonderful it would have been, she thought, to start a relationship with him from scratch, without the excess baggage of disapproving ancestors.

The day she had first rummaged through that pair of steamer trunks belonging to her great-aunt Renae, Lindsay had told herself that twenty-six was too old to be developing a grand passion such as the one Renae had felt for Nils. Now she knew she had been mistaken. Erik was everything she had ever wanted in a man. Competent, generous, kind, handsome, devoted. . . .

Very devoted to his family, she reminded herself glumly. Did he intend to let the opinions of his relatives keep them apart forever?

Erik had long since put aside any notion of choosing a bride from a background similar to his own. He hadn't known her long, but he knew the woman he wanted.

Roses in full bloom perfumed the velvety spring night as he escorted Lindsay up to her front porch and drew her close. Her eyes, as she looked up at him, were so luminous they seemed to have trapped the moonlight within them. He bent his head, tracing his lips across the softness of hers and thinking he'd never tasted anything so sweet.

"Lin. Darling, Lin. . . ."

"Umm, Erik. . . ."

Lindsay's head was spinning, her senses aflame. Reveling in Erik's powerful embrace, she curled her fingers up through his thick, blond hair and kissed him back with all the ardor she'd been saving up for years just in case she ever met the man of her dreams.

Now that she'd found him, she didn't want to let go.

"Lin, sweet Lin. I've never known anyone like you."

The anguished murmur seemed to have been dragged from the depths of his being. Soft and ragged as it was, it hit Lindsay's ears like a wake-up alarm. Snapping out of the romantic trance she'd fallen into, she put some distance between them, an inch at a time, until her heartbeat had resumed its normal pace.

No, she thought as the moonlight in her eyes turned slick with the sheen of tears, he never had known anyone like her. And that was the problem. In spite of this incredible attraction, they still didn't have a single thing in common!

In the weeks since resigning from Denim Ala Mode, Lindsay had learned firsthand how expensive and chancy starting a new business could be. No salary was coming in, while insurance, fees, and display materials had taken huge chunks out of her savings.

"Don't expect an immediate rush of customers," Addie warned, trying to spare her disappointment.

Lindsay knew she didn't dare be overoptimistic on that score. "A trickle is what I'll get if I'm lucky. Maybe not even that unless I can find some way to let the public know that Gladrags is about to be launched!"

Unfortunately, she couldn't afford a nickel for advertising. Worse yet, the driveway was sadly in need of resurfacing. Even though she'd learned to slow down when wheeling onto the graveled path, her van had several times lurched into potholes with a force sufficient to jar loose the windshield wipers. Addie had formed the prudent habit of parking down the street in front of the Jensens' house. But they couldn't keep that up for long, and paying customers could hardly be expected to cope with such primitive parking conditions.

Almost in despair Lindsay made a special trip to the attic. There she spent a whole morning rummaging through boxes and cartons so thickly coated with dust they had clearly not been touched in at least three-quarters of a century. What she hoped to find was another board game collectible enough to bring in enough quick cash to cover the price of patched asphalt.

What she found was better than that. Much better.

In the past Lindsay had always paid her own way. She didn't believe in letting her escorts bear the whole brunt of the cost of dating. Erik was more old-fashioned than her former boyfriends in that regard, however. He got a bit insulted when she attempted to split the check. Rather than squabble, Lindsay had given in and learned to graciously accept being treated to dinner and the movies and now and then an afternoon of sailing or horseback riding.

But this time she had a real coup to celebrate. She decided to treat him to an evening out and to make it a night to remember.

A well-timed phone call caught him at lunch. Making sure he understood that he was to be her guest, she issued a dinner invitation, asking him to pick her up at six-thirty. Then she phoned and made reservations at the famous old Benbow Inn, located about a half hour's drive south of Ferndale.

Remembering Erik's comments about appreciating extra-feminine "girl clothes," Lindsay chose her wardrobe for the night with him in mind. "Gonna knock his socks off," she planned happily, slithering into a fringed and beaded flapper dress.

A glance in the mirror made her crow in delight. Her image seemed to have taken on a syncopated shimmer from the dazzling burnt-orange gown designed by Vionnet.

She rolled on a pair of mist-fine McCallum evening hosiery that had somehow survived the decades, then stepped into high, high heels with taut toes and superarched insteps. The spectacular dress needed little ornamentation. The single strand of waist-length beads was chosen more as a prop than anything.

Bobbed hair, Lindsay knew, was almost essential to complete the twenties look. She wasn't about to go that far in impersonating an "It Girl." But by drawing poufs of hair forward over her ears and pinning the rest of it securely to the nape of her neck, she managed to achieve a semblance of that sleek, cropped appearance she wanted.

When the door knocker clattered at six-thirty, she ankled to the edge of the foyer.

"Come on in!"

Erik was wearing her favorite outfit, the costume that always made her think of him as a charro, one of those dashing cowboys from the "Californio" days before the Gold Rush. As he stepped through the door, Lindsay slouched toward him twirling the long strand of beads, like a campy old star of the silver screen.

She had expected the generally unflappable Erik to exclaim "Holy Theda Bara!" and burst out laughing. Instead, his bronzed face paled.

"That's you, Lin, right?" he choked, ignoring her slump-shouldered vampishness.

Lindsay felt a jab of annoyance. She'd gone to a lot of trouble to emulate Clara

Bow or one of Valentino's leading ladies. The least Erik could have done was play along.

Maybe it would have helped if she'd hunted up a long, enameled cigarette holder. "Who else would it be, for heaven's sake?" she demanded in disgust.

Then it hit her what the problem was. To her, Renae was a girl from the past who'd had an unhappy romance, died young, and left trunks full of gorgeous clothes behind. It was easy — convenient — to forget that to Erik, Renae was still around. The very first day they'd met, he'd insisted that he'd been bumping into her for years, every time he went near the gazebo!

Erik felt foolish, allowing the sight of a pretty young flapper to shake him up like that. That dress was dynamite, though Lindsay was curvier than a girl of the twenties would have been. Every other detail was perfect. Good grief, she even had Vaseline on her eyelids!

"Sorry," he apologized stiffly. "You just took me by surprise."

He didn't have to tell her *that!* "That old family resemblance rearing its ugly head?"

Erik's jaw clenched. "At least I didn't fall off a ladder this time."

"So you *did* think I was Renae!" By now

Lindsay regretted having started this whole thing. Why hadn't she worn a hobble skirt or a prom dress from the fifties? A heart-sick anger caused her to say more than she'd intended.

"It must have been quite a disappointment to realize it was only me instead of your melancholy ghost," she snapped, turning away in a huff. "Pardon me while I go change. I just figured that since you're so wrapped up in the past, you might appreciate —"

Erik grabbed her by the arm and swung her back around. "Shut up, Lin!"

He enforced the command with a kiss that took her breath away. She struggled for a second or two out of shock, then felt emotion taking her around in a spiral. What a Looney Tunes she was, acting jealous over his attachment to a poor, sad girl from the past when all she really wanted to do was build a future with him.

Jerking back, she snatched a breath. "Do you always growl at women when you're about to kiss them?"

"No. Only before I propose."

Erik's expression was strained but as determined as she'd ever seen it. Though he made no attempt to pull her back against his chest, he circled her wrist with his iron-strong fingers to prevent her escape.

"Sorry, Lin," he apologized huskily. "I guess I should have picked a more romantic setting when I asked you to marry me. But things got out of hand, and I lost my head. It was bound to happen sooner or later. That's just one of the reasons it's not a good idea to wait any longer. Let's get married. Right away."

Chapter Seven

Lindsay couldn't decide whether to feel flattered or to burst into tears. She'd been proposed to before — several times. None of her other suitors had tried to rush her to the altar, however, and all of them had said something sweet about being in love with her.

Her dark, winged brows lifted. "Right away? Don't you think that's rather hasty, Erik?"

He threw back a challenge in place of an answer. "Can you deny there's been something between us from the beginning?"

She shrugged uncomfortably. Had he felt it too, then? It was as if some invisible bond kept drawing her to him. But their heritage stood in the way. Those skeletons rattling around in both their closets.

"There have been times when I've thought about our ancestors and wondered if you and I had a chance to make up for all the happiness they missed out on," she admitted. "Then I remember the feud. It's still not over, you know. Not while at least one person in your family is carrying a grudge about something that happened half a century before we were born!"

The shot went home. Erik flushed and abruptly released her wrist. "What an accusation! You don't even know my Uncle Olin!"

"Whose fault is that?" She tossed the question at him like a firecracker. "I assumed you hadn't introduced us because you knew he'd disapprove of your associating with a da Silva. Think how he'd feel if you married one!" Suddenly one explanation for that hasty proposal occurred to her. "Had you planned to present your family with a fait accompli so they wouldn't have a chance to talk you out of it?"

He didn't know who he felt angrier at, himself for starting the whole thing, or Lindsay for accusing him of such a devious maneuver.

"Call me superstitious if you like, but I was afraid if we waited, something might happen to separate us forever too," he declared. "You know what happened the last time a Thorvaldsen and a da Silva decided to get married."

"Yes." Lindsay caught her breath, wondering how it would have felt to be loved the way Nils loved Renae. If she had tossed caution to the winds and taken Erik up on his proposal, would she have found out?

He glared at her, fighting down the impulse to toss her over his shoulder and march off for a visit to a ship captain he knew who was empowered to perform marriages. "I figured that once we were partners, we'd have the rest of our lives to stomp out the effects of that rotten feud, to make mighty sure it wouldn't affect another generation."

He was talking about their children, Lindsay realized. What would their offspring be like? Fair? Dark? Or a combination of both Thorvaldsen and da Silva characteristics?

"I'm sorry, Erik," she apologized. "It's just that I've heard so much about your uncle that I've grown a little paranoid about him." She reached out and squeezed his solid, workman's hand. "Hopefully we can do something about ending the feud forever, but it's not a good idea to rush, or — or jump into something for all the wrong reasons."

Erik took his hand back and resisted the impulse to clench his fist as he shoved it into his pocket. He had never proposed to anyone before, and he wouldn't have done it so abruptly if he hadn't been so startled by seeing her standing there in that incredible costume. Nevertheless, it rankled that she'd turned him down without seeming to think twice about the rejection.

"What do you mean — 'for all the wrong reasons'?" he growled.

Lindsay gestured vaguely. "Oh, you know. Because we got to feeling sentimental about the fact that the romance between Nils and Renae ended so sadly. Or. . . . Well, it doesn't really matter. We ought to be going, don't you think? Just give me a minute to run up and change."

"There's no need to put on anything else. That outfit looks great."

"It'll only take a minute," Lindsay insisted and was up the stairs before he could argue.

The orange dress was spectacular, she agreed as she caught sight of it in the mirror of her room. But the news she'd put it on to celebrate now seemed like an anticlimax. Besides. . . .

A bit unwillingly she took another look at the reflection in the glass and pictured a slightly younger woman with bobbed hair standing there. Was that why Erik had proposed like that, right out of the blue? Because he'd been in love with Renae for years and years and years, and when *she'd*

163

shown up in a dress straight out of the twenties, he simply couldn't keep his feelings to himself?

Angry and disappointed, Lindsay jerked her most up-to-the-minute ensemble out of the closet and zipped herself up. She wasn't about to play stand-in for a melancholy ghost!

Later, over coffee, when her hurt feelings had started to mend, Lindsay shared her good news with her escort.

"Tomorrow a paving company will be out to resurface the driveway," she confided. "What's more, there'll be a big notice in all the area newspapers next week, advertising our grand opening."

"Win the lottery, did you?"

It was a relief to hear his teasing tone. Erik couldn't have been particularly disappointed at her response to his proposal, Lindsay assured herself.

"Nope. I found a Leap Frog bank for Mrs. Butler's collection," she said jubilantly and recounted her brief meeting with Addie's customer several weeks earlier. "She was buying a Jonah and the Whale bank that time. It cost four hundred dollars."

Erik's brows shot up. "Are you talking about an ordinary child's penny bank?"

"Not so ordinary," Lindsay said with a laugh. "Mechanical banks were all the rage around the turn of the century, but there weren't all that many of any one kind made, and not all those were good, by any means. Over the space of a hundred years, most of them probably wound up in the trash. Anyway, that day in Eureka Addie mentioned keeping an eye out for a Leap Frog bank, but I had honestly forgotten all about that. I was shaking Indian head pennies out of this one when I brought it in to show Addie this afternoon. She nearly fainted when she saw me jiggling it up and down."

"What's so special about it?"

"Well, it's rare, for one thing." Lindsay explained that the Leap Frog mechanical bank was a cast-iron toy made by Shepard Hardware in 1891. "Even the paint on the one I found was still in great condition. Addie had some facts on file showing that one like it but in only average condition sold a year ago for $4,400."

"For a kid's *toy?*"

"For a collector's item," Lindsay emphasized. "But yes, isn't it amazing? Mrs. Butler offered $4,700 for the bank sight unseen, then made it all the way down from Eureka in under half an hour to pick it up. She was just delighted, Erik, and so am I. It's going to be *great* to have that driveway fixed!"

By the time they left the restaurant, her bubbling enthusiasm had fizzed away. The ride home was one long, awkward pause. At the curb in front of her house, Lindsay self-consciously got out her keys.

"Thank you for dinner," he said. "I enjoyed it."

Her marshmallow heart went out to him when she heard the flat tone. "Erik," she said with a catch in her voice, "you took me by surprise a while ago. I wouldn't want you to think. . . . We're good friends, you and I, and —" Darn! How could she say she was sorry for turning him down flat? "Later, when Gladrags is off the ground, could we maybe discuss the future again?"

In the dwindling twilight Erik's Scandinavian face looked almost remote. "I'm the one who should apologize for not timing things better," he said, taking the blame onto his own shoulders. "Usually I don't get carried away and open my big mouth without considering all sides of a question. Frankly, Lin, I don't think there's any point in talking about the future until we've straightened out the past."

For all the rest she got that night, Lindsay might as well have stretched out on a bed of nails. Pinpricks of guilt jabbed sharply at her, keeping her from closing her eyes without remembering Erik's parting words.

She had never followed through on her promise to help try to locate the letters he believed Nils must have written to Renae. After one all-day effort, her fascination with the vintage clothing up in the attic had drawn her concentration away from the search.

There was something else she'd neglected too, Lindsay reminded herself. The first time she'd passed that old summerhouse, she'd felt a strange, sad loneliness about the place. But never since had she gone down to the creek with an open mind in an effort to investigate Erik's claim that the gazebo was haunted.

It had been all too easy to keep postponing that foray. She'd been busy. And suppose Erik was right about the spirit of her Great-Aunt Renae sticking close to home all these years? What could she do about it, anyway?

Erik, she thought. That's what it all boiled down to. He insisted that since he was a little boy, he'd been catching sight of Renae da Silva. He wanted to do something for Renae; find out the truth and set her free. It was important to him. So important that when she'd talked about the future, he'd snapped something about straightening out the past first.

As soon as the shop was launched, she'd buckle down and give the house a thorough searching, Lindsay resolved. And the minute she could afford to do so, she'd see about tearing down that shabby old gazebo.

Oddly enough, that notion made her feel guiltier than ever.

He had a lot of nerve, needling her about resolving the past before making plans for the future, Erik heckled himself. Who was the turkey that had tried to ignore the heritage of both their families by pulling something downright underhanded? If Lindsay ever found out, she wouldn't reconsider her answer to his proposal. In fact, she'd probably never speak to him again!

Not that his action hadn't been justified. In a way, at least. Including such a discriminatory clause in her will was like flapping a red tablecloth at a bull, and Felice da Silva must have known that perfectly well when she wrote it. But that didn't give him the right to take her aunt's stiff-necked attitude out on Lindsay. She wasn't responsible for the old woman's prejudices, any more than he was to blame for his great-uncle's bias against the da Silvas.

Anger and resentment at both their families went into the next few nails Erik drove. Lindsay's comments had made it clear that his delay in introducing her to Uncle Olin hadn't gone unnoticed. He'd intended to bring them together, of course, long before this. But something always came up to interfere.

Yeah, he jibed at himself. *Cowardice. You're dying to have them like each other, and you know that such a thing happening is a million-to-one shot. But you can't look the other way and pretend that old feud doesn't really affect you, Thorvaldsen. Not if you hope to convince Lindsay that your reasons for wanting to marry her are the right ones.*

The new driveway was a joy to behold, Lindsay and Addie agreed. They pooled their spare cash to insert midweek ads in all the area newspapers, announcing the joint grand opening of Gladrags and Beautiful Dreamer.

The appearance of the eye-catching ad gave Erik the opportunity he'd been hoping for. He phoned Lindsay on Thursday morning and asked her out for the evening. She had accepted before learning that what he had in mind wasn't a tête-à-tête. In fact, the confrontation was more than likely to be a good, old-fashioned head-to-head. His Great-Uncle Olin was coming along!

It was impossible for Lindsay not to remember Karin's description of her own first meeting with the Thorvaldsen family patriarch. "He feels duty-bound to pass approval on anyone his great-nieces and -nephews choose to marry. Before deciding that I would probably fit in all right, he did a lot of grumbling about my ancestry being Norwegian instead of Danish."

But at least Karin's family had originated in Scandinavia. What about someone whose maternal bloodlines stretched back into Portugal? Lindsay gave a discouraged groan. As Erik had commented at the very beginning, their two families didn't have a single thing in common!

For the first time in her life, she found herself wishing she were a blue-eyed blonde like Erik's three sisters-in-law. Just temporarily, of course. Just long enough to pass muster with Uncle Olin.

She knew now that had it not been for the long-standing enmity between their two families, her reaction to the proposal would have been entirely different. She would have accepted — wholeheartedly. By now she would have been proudly wearing an engagement ring from the man she loved.

I do love Erik, she acknowledged with a wistful sigh. *Maybe I have from the very beginning, when I saw him tangled up in that ladder.*

But it wasn't just the past that had to be straightened out, Lindsay knew. She was going to have to learn to coexist peacefully with all the Thorvaldsens. Especially the oldest one.

Her own best clothing tended to be short-skirted, bright-hued outfits that flattered her neat figure and dramatic coloring. For this first meeting Lindsay decided to play it safe. One of the attic trunks had yielded up a treasure trove of softly feminine fashions from the late 1940s. From among this ladylike wardrobe she chose a demure teal-blue suit, whose full skirt swirled to midcalf length. The suit's short, snug jacket buttoned to the throat, while in the back, a dainty peplum gave the appear-

171

ance of a mini-bustle.

The accessories she selected to wear with this classic ensemble were equally prim. Nevertheless, the moment she opened the front door that evening, Lindsay had the sinking feeling that for the second time in a row she'd made the wrong choice when it came to picking out something to wear. The elderly man standing on the step beside Erik stiffened in disapproval as his faded blue eyes noted every detail of her appearance.

Too late, it occurred to Lindsay that the pretty suit had probably belonged to Felice, his longtime enemy. The look on Olin Thorvaldsen's face made it quite evident that though his hair might be white and his face seamed, his memory was as sharp as ever.

"How nice to meet you," she lied with determination when Erik performed introductions. "Won't you come in for a moment while I get my things?"

"Thank you, no."

The stubborn expression told her even more than his words. Though he had agreed to come along since it seemed so important to his great-nephew, he had no intention of setting foot inside the da Silva home!

Tactfully Erik interjected the information that they had reservations at Filini's North in fifteen minutes.

Lindsay forced a smile. "How nice. I always enjoy seeing Marta. And Tony is a marvelous chef, don't you agree, Mr. Thorvaldsen?"

"For someone who favors sauces over smorgasbörg," he conceded. "But what can you expect? He's from the city."

And Italian, Lindsay thought astutely. She wondered if the old man really preferred pickled herring to Veal Marsala, or if he was only making waves out of habit.

"Well, so am I," she replied, trying to keep her tone placid. "But now we've both moved to Ferndale. It's a lovely little town."

"It is," he agreed. "For dairy farmers."

Erik's square jaw tightened. This was ridiculous! After his uncle had finally agreed to come and meet Lindsay, he'd figured he had a fighting chance of relegating the past to the niche where it belonged. With another woman, it might have worked. But Olin had taken one look at Lindsay and turned into a starched old martinet who'd apparently forgotten what courtesy was all about.

Sandwiched between the two men in the

cab of the truck, Lindsay felt Erik's shoulder tense. She heard him suck in a quick, angry breath, and suspected that he was about to jump to her defense. That was the last thing she needed, she thought. If she intended to live peacefully in this town, she would have to win Olin over herself. And do it quickly!

She remembered a Russian envoy who had nearly driven her father crazy before the American diplomat had stumbled across the key to getting along with his opposite number.

"Ah, but if everyone were a dairy farmer, there would be too many cows and far too much competition for the cream dollar," said Peter Dorsett's daughter in a calm, reasonable tone. "They'd swing the local economy into a recession. I imagine there are plenty of nervous farmers around here, anyway, what with all the emphasis lately on low cholesterol and fat-free food."

Out of the corner of his eye, Erik observed his great-uncle's reaction to Lindsay's tongue-in-cheek response. He'd half expected the old man to take offense. Instead, Olin looked mildly surprised at having been challenged.

"Humph!" he sniffed. "Those diet-fad people are doing their darnedest to take all the joy out of living."

"Uh-huh," Lindsay agreed. "Just imagine what they'd do if we said we lived in *Butterfat* mansions!"

Faded or not, Olin Thorvaldsen's eyes had a lively twinkle in them. "Health-food nuts!" he grumbled, his disdain aimed at that group of picky eaters rather than at the dark-haired young woman who was the image of that young flapper his brother Nils had adored.

By the time they reached the restaurant, the tension inside the truck had eased considerably. It started up again, however, the instant they walked inside Filini's North. Not only was Marta wearing a high-necked gown that had once belonged to Luzia da Silva, but an eye-catching sign near the front entrance announced that the hostess's wardrobe was furnished by Gladrags!

"Secondhand clothes!" Uncle Olin rumbled. "Most undignified profession I ever heard of. At least that Tony fellow cooks. Why are you wasting your time with a lot of old rags?"

Lindsay realized that she had a long way to go if she hoped to ever get along with this opinionated old man. She could grovel, knuckle under — or stand up for her beliefs and risk the consequences.

"For the same reason archaeologists get down on their hands and knees to sift through the dirt in hopes of finding broken shards of pottery that will give them some clues about ancient civilizations," she answered firmly. "Chippendale furniture made long before the Revolution is worth many times what its modern-day replicas sell for. That's partly because when we look at one of those old tables or chests of drawers, we think about the important things that were happening in the world at the time it was made. I consider clothing a part of our history too. It can teach us a great deal about the way people lived and what sort of things went on in a particular era to influence the way men and women dressed."

Olin's furrowed face grew thoughtful. "Never thought of that," he admitted. "Wouldn't be surprised if you weren't partly right. Take that getup you've got on, for instance. It's not the sort of thing a lady would wear if she was coping with ration books and a victory garden and worrying about whether someone she loved would come safely home from overseas."

"That's right!" Lindsay bobbed her head enthusiastically. "Styles like these came in just a couple of years after the end of

World War II. They were made for women like Rosie the Riveter and all those Army nurses who served in the war zones. After all those hard years, it must have been wonderful to have a chance to get dressed up and look pretty again."

Passing a plate of antipasto around the table, Erik marveled that so much significance could be woven into a few yards of fabric. More miraculous yet was the reaction Lindsay had managed to coax out of his stubborn old relative. He'd have said that his uncle never had a thought in his head that didn't concern cream production. Now it turned out he was sort of a nostalgia buff. Amazing!

"Day after tomorrow is the grand opening of Lindsay's new shop," Erik casually remarked. "Doing anything special that day, Uncle Olin? If not, how about dropping by with me to see more of those old-time clothes that have lessons about the past stitched into every seam?"

He hadn't promised to come, Lindsay reminded herself two days later. Olin Thorvaldsen had dodged giving a direct answer as adroitly as a wily politician evading a question about when he was going to keep his campaign promises. She had a feeling the biggest stumbling block had more to do with entering the traditional home of the da Silvas than with vintage clothing.

Whatever the cause, two o'clock had already come and gone with no sign of either Erik or his great-uncle. Fortunately, she thought with a twinge of gratitude, not all the Thorvaldsens were so standoffish. Early that morning Erik's sisters-in-law had arrived to set up coffee urns on picnic tables out on the patio. They had filled her refrigerator with trays of finger sandwiches, tea cakes, and garden-fresh vegetables to be dunked into a cheesy dip.

"Nobody is allowed near the food until they've spent at least twenty minutes shopping," Shelby declared with a wide grin.

"Absolutely," Ingrid backed her up. "All my friends are coming, and they've been warned. Buy first, eat afterward!"

Karin had turned to Lindsay with a concerned expression. "Have you a spot where people can go to try things on? A woman I know at work has always longed to swathe herself in one of those luxurious feather-trimmed negligees like Carole Lombard and Jean Harlow wore in the thirties movies. There's something on the rack over there that would be just perfect for her."

Lindsay felt genuinely touched by their support. Their friends and acquaintances did show up, and quite a few of them made purchases. Sometimes only a knickknack, a strip of old lace, or an interesting assortment of buttons to trim an item they themselves were sewing. Sometimes, like Karin's coworker, a piece of period lingerie or the Amelia Earhart style jacket that Ingrid's cousin found irresistible.

Personal invitations to attend the grand opening had been mailed to all of Beautiful Dreamer's Old Town clientele. The attendance was also swelled by droves of antique hunters responding to the newspaper advertisements.

"Bless Mrs. Butler for buying that old bank!" Lindsay slumped into a nineteenth-century chair for a brief rest after saying good-bye to a group from Garberville. "Nowhere near this many people would have shown up without the ads her money paid for."

"No, or gotten out of the driveway with their wheels intact, either. Oh-oh, look who's here," Addie said, getting wearily to her feet again as a pair of young professionals turned up the walk. "My former landlords."

"They did us both a big favor by evicting

you," Lindsay reminded her with a giggle. She, too, got up, and went to welcome Clayton and Eva Simms.

Being owners of an antique house themselves, the lawyers were interested in every detail of Lindsay's mansion. With knowledgeable looks they inspected the elegant marble fireplaces and nineteenth-century wallpaper in the parlors turned showrooms, then bought an old rosewood chest from Addie before spotting friends on the patio and joining them there for refreshments.

New footsteps echoed in the entry hall. Lindsay summoned a businesslike smile. It turned into a genuine warm glow of welcome when she saw first Erik and then his great-uncle appear in the doorway.

"I'm so pleased you could come!" Moving forward, she held out her hand to Olin Thorvaldsen. It was a shame, she thought, that this scene couldn't have been played out generations earlier. What a lot of heartbreak that would have saved both families!

"Sorry we couldn't get here sooner." Erik would never have told Lindsay about the hours of agonizing vacillation his great-uncle had gone through before bringing himself to cross the da Silva threshold. But he had a feeling she might have guessed what a hard decision it was for the old man to make. "How has it been going?"

"Wonderfully well." Lindsay assured herself that the exuberant joy she felt had nothing to do with the fact that Erik was standing next to her. Even so, it was thrilling to reflect that together the two of them might have succeeded in ending a seventy-year-old feud. "I've sold oodles of accessories plus some of the Victorian whites and three dainty little girls' dresses. They were made from nainsook and trimmed with yards of ribbon. Oh, plus a swansdown wrapper Marlene Dietrich would have looked absolutely devastating in."

"Sounds like Gladrags is off to a rousing start."

"Yes, and Addie is having a red-letter day too." Lindsay would have taken his great-uncle's arm and conducted him on a personally escorted tour. Ingrid bustled up just then, however, and lured him into the next room to look at the unusual collection of malacca walking sticks Lindsay had accumulated.

"Thank you for bringing him," she said, smiling up at Erik. "I'll bet it was like pulling teeth to persuade him to come."

"Wisdom teeth," Erik conceded. "But I don't think there'll be any problems from now on."

"I hope not." Lindsay gave his hand a happy squeeze. Everything was starting to work out just beautifully! Granted, they had never learned what happened to Nils, but suddenly the future seemed bright despite that gloomy past that had clouded the lives of their ancestors.

Before she could put these feelings into words, she caught sight of a familiar face in the next room. "Excuse me for a minute, will you, Erik? I want to say hello to Mrs. Butler before she and Addie get engrossed in talking about old toys."

Erik's bemused gaze followed Lindsay as she slipped across the hall to Beautiful Dreamer's section of the premises. The sight of her in a sunny yellow walking dress from 1919 made him think of another war that had ended long ago and the way peoples' joyous reaction to peace was reflected in their choice of clothing.

Suddenly a hand descended onto his shoulder. He looked around to find Clayton Simms beaming at him. The lawyer was a close friend of his eldest brother, Knud. He and Eva had been handling the Thorvaldsen family's legal matters ever since they'd passed their bar exams a few years back.

"We were hoping to run into you today," Clayton said jovially, adding that it was all too seldom that they had a chance to visit Ferndale. "Do you still anticipate beginning on our remodel around the twenty-fifth of the month?"

Erik nodded his assurance. Under ordinary circumstances he would have chosen to postpone the Eureka job until September at the earliest, but a deal was a deal. Within days of striking the bargain with Clayton, he had changed his mind about having the attorney follow through on what he had asked him to do. Nevertheless, he felt obliged to honor his word.

"Everything's right on schedule," he confirmed. "Matter of fact, the permits have already been issued."

"We're both thrilled at the prospect."

Clayton's attention was attracted by the domed, Roman-style Tiffany chandelier suspended from the twelve-foot ceiling. He threw back his head to study the antique lighting fixture more closely.

"Every detail of this place is downright stupendous," he declared, blinking as he refocused on the younger man. "I can sure understand why you were so eager to acquire the mansion last spring that you asked me to check into ways of circumventing that will."

A gasp from behind them brought both men wheeling around. Erik fell his heart take a nosedive. Well within earshot stood a slender, black-haired young woman attired in an old-fashioned, sunshine-yellow gown.

But the expression on her face resembled a declaration of war!

Chapter Eight

Somehow Lindsay made it through the rest of the afternoon with her smile intact. It was a forced, determined smile, however; occasional reflections on *Thelma and Louise*, a bizarre movie about revenge that she had seen a year or so earlier, rippled through her mind whenever she considered the perfidy of Erik Thorvaldsen.

At least he hadn't tried to exonerate himself on the spot. "I'm sorry, Lin. I promise to explain later," he'd murmured after seeing her standing behind him like a victim of shellshock following the bombshell his attorney had dropped. "It's not quite as bad as Clay made it sound, but I'm hardly blameless. We need privacy to hash it out, though. That — and a lot of other things."

What other things? Lindsay wondered, seething. If he thought she'd be inclined to talk about the future with him *now* — She spun around and left him standing there. But twenty minutes later there was no way she could ignore his uncle. Not without starting that wretched old feud all over again.

"Good-bye, my dear." With Erik hovering in the background, Olin proceeded toward her at a careful, arthritic pace. "I apologize for calling your business undignified. I can see now that it's nothing of the sort. Will you come to lunch soon and allow me to return the hospitality you've shown us today? I'd be pleased to have you sample some of the excellent cheeses we make at our dairy."

Generations of Dorsetts had been renowned for diplomacy. Not about to be outdone in savoir faire, Lindsay replied that she would be honored to come, while leaving the date open. She wouldn't refuel the feud. Certainly not! However, she intended to make sure that the cheese-tasting took place at a time when Olin's great-nephew was marooned on a distant roof.

"Good-bye." She waved them off. "Thank you again for coming."

The gilt banjo clock in the entry hall was chiming six when the Thorvaldsens took their leave. Most of the other antiquers had departed by then too, although two customers lingered another half hour. Then there were dust sheets to drape across delicate merchandise and the day's proceeds to tally. Lindsay had just waved good-bye to Addie when the phone rang.

A surge of emotion caught in her throat when she heard Erik's voice. She was angry — very angry — at what certainly seemed to have been an underhanded attempt on his part to flaunt her great-aunt's final wishes by purchasing the da Silva mansion through his friend's clandestine assistance.

The temptation to slam the receiver down was almost overpowering. Then Lindsay remembered how terrible she'd felt after shutting him out once before. Erik had asked her to marry him. Much to her regret, she'd refused. Now he was asking her to listen to an explanation. She didn't want to spend the rest of her life sorrowing over what might have been.

"Go ahead, Erik," she said in as steady a tone as she could manage. "I'm listening."

"Lin, you have every right to be furious at me," Erik said contritely. "Believe it or not, I'm actually relieved that Clay Simms let the cat out of the bag. That under-the-table deal has been on my conscience from the start, even though I pulled out of that side of the bargain only a couple of days after I set it up."

Lindsay brushed aside a tear that was plowing a path down her cheek. He had been perfectly open about wanting to buy the house at first, she admitted. It was only after hearing about Aunt Felice's will that he'd resorted to that bit of chicanery.

"That's the reason Addie was evicted on such short notice, isn't it?" she asked heatedly. "What did you do, move up the remodel of the Simms house in exchange for advice on shifty tactics in acquiring my property?"

"Yup. That's exactly what I did." Erik faced the music. He cleared his throat. "Look, Lin, I wouldn't have hurt your feelings for every Victorian mansion on the north coast put together. But I want you to remember that I wasn't trying to hornswoggle you out of your house. Back in April you had every intention of returning to San Francisco. You were going to sell the place to *somebody*. What was the first thing a new owner would have done?"

Lindsay didn't have to think very hard to come up with that answer. "Torn down that awful old derelict of a gazebo, of course. Oh! Is that why —"

"All these years it's been the only thing she's had," he said simply. "Lin, I've got this cast-iron hunch that together we can find out what Renae needs to know to let her rest peacefully. Look — the phone is no way to discuss something like this. We need to sit down and hash it out face to face."

"Nose to nose?" The sound of his voice had soothed her outraged feelings to the point where she could manage a small joke.

"Cheek to cheek, lips to lips, heart to heart," he declared in anything but a joking tone. "I'd be there right now except that something's gone haywire with the truck's engine. I'm stuck out here at Uncle Olin's until I can get it fixed," he chaffed. "But I'll make it back into town tonight if I have to saddle up one of his cows to get there."

The whimsical suggestion pried a small giggle from Lindsay. "And I thought *I* had trouble with traffic cops! Better not risk it, Erik. We'll talk tomorrow."

She had a feeling that only the need to get back and tinker with the insides of the truck kept him from arguing the matter further. Wearily she headed upstairs to change out of the charming, old-fashioned dress she had worn for Gladrags's grand opening.

Once she understood Erik's reason for

that sneaky deal he and Clay Simms had tried to pull, her hurt anger had turned to understanding. She and Erik hadn't even known each other for an hour, she remembered, before he was putting up a sincere defense of the gazebo.

He cared about people, she thought, and reminded herself what a rare quality that was in this day and age. Most of the men and women of her acquaintance were concerned only with themselves and with getting ahead; until very recently she would have had to number herself right up there with them. But Erik . . . he was one of the unselfish ones. His family meant a great deal to him. So would his wife, when in the future some woman was sensible enough to accept his proposal. So did a young woman who had died nearly seven decades ago, even though she was on the opposite side of the barricades in the Thorvaldsen/da Silva feud.

Renae was *her* relative, Lindsay thought ruefully. But except for that one futile search, she'd never done anything to try to set her to rest. Only the letters could do that. And they might never be found.

Unless. . . .

In the Art Deco mirror, Lindsay caught sight of the misty outlines of the gazebo floating in the glass.

"She'd know where the letters are," she murmured to the astonished-looking young woman in the glass who still hadn't even decided if she believed in ghosts. "They were hers, after all."

She gulped. "Why don't I ask her where she put them?"

From a slight distance, the summer-house looked cheery and gay, like a horse-less merry-go-round or a hot-air balloon a little too tipsy for flight. Up close, however, the rollicking glee that had seemed a part of the aged structure was replaced by a somber atmosphere. Approaching through the back orchard, Lindsay had the conviction that more than the gloomy, graying twilight gave the creekside gazebo its air of hopeless desolation.

She shivered as a glacierlike chill touched her skin. Clenching her jaw to quiet her chattering teeth, Lindsay resisted the strong, panicky impulse to turn and run. Instead, she set a foot on the bottom step and paused. Looking around. Seeing nobody but sure — oh, so sure — that someone was staring back.

"R-R-Renae?"

The name was hardly more than a

quaver. Taking a reinforcing breath, Lindsay tried again. "Renae, I'm the last of your family. The only one left with da Silva blood in her veins. We're kin, you and I. We look a lot alike, I think. And — and we both love a man named Thorvaldsen. You've seen Erik. He's Nils's great-nephew."

Cricket chirps ceased. Frogs stopped croaking. Even the fast-flowing ripples seemed to swirl along the surface of the creek on tiptoe.

Taking the intensified silence as encouragement, Lindsay climbed the rest of the way up to the warped, weathered platform. Built up from the edges of the low wall, circular benches seemed almost to spin in the air through centrifugal force. Overhead, the weathered domed roof swayed on its unsteady supports.

The aged wood creaked and groaned as she proceeded to the center, then halted. She had a strong feeling that she was being watched, but sharp glances in all directions showed not so much as a robin in view. Yet the sense of audience grew more acute with each moment.

"Erik and I are trying to find out what happened to Nils," she explained aloud. "We hope to trace him through the return address on his letters. He *did* write to you, didn't he, Renae?"

Silence. Nothing. It was like talking into a vacuum. Doggedly, Lindsay continued.

"People who knew you when . . . before . . . told Erik that you and Nils were never really happy unless you could be together. The long separations your families forced on you must have made you both miserable, especially since I don't suppose you could even talk on the phone long distance very often. But we're sure you must have kept in touch by mail. For a while, at least. Then . . . what happened, Renae'? Did the letters stop coming?"

A doleful breeze keened through the branches.

"Weeping won't help!" Lindsay cried impatiently, forgetting for a moment that the person to whom she spoke had mourned herself to death on this very spot. "We need your help to prove that Nils would have come back if something hadn't prevented him from doing so. With your letters, we have a chance of ending that wretched feud between the Thorvaldsens and the da Silvas once and for all. What did you do with them?"

The creek waters lay low, hibernating. The breeze died. Not the flutter of a leaf or the drone of a mosquito ruffled the tension-filled air.

Lindsay's temper snapped. "Maybe you don't *want* to know what happened to Nils. Is that it, Renae? Did the last letter that arrived from him say he didn't love you anymore? Tell you that he'd found another girl back East —"

A stinging wind rose out of nowhere and slapped the words right out of her mouth. Before she could catch her breath, she was engulfed in a mini-cyclone buzzing around her like a swarm of angry hornets.

Terrified by the brutal assault, Lindsay threw up her hands to cover her eyes. She managed a gasp of protest. "Stop it, Renae! Don't vent your rage on me. Help us learn the truth! Where are the letters?"

For an endless minute longer, the gale-force buffeting rampaged on. Lashed by the ferocity of the storm, Lindsay's long black hair whipped from side to side. Her clothes fluttered furiously, the sizzling energy in the air threatening to rip the cloth apart thread by thread. Stumbling blindly toward the steps, Lindsay reached out in self-defense as the double page of a newspaper sailed at her like an airborne manta ray.

The wind's battering onslaught ebbed as

her fingers closed over the limp, serrated edge of the sheet of newsprint.

Pulse racing from the incredible ordeal she'd just been through, Lindsay jumped down off the platform. She didn't believe that newspaper had landed on her by chance, any more than she believed the sudden, violent wind had been a natural quirk of climate.

Scarcely enough twilight remained to enable her to make out the smudged black print. According to the masthead information, the paper had been printed months earlier in Grants Pass, Oregon, a town far north of Ferndale. Limp, beginning to yellow, it was the sort of debris no one would look at twice.

"Why did you send me this?" Lindsay complained. "It's nothing but an old ad from a furniture store!"

With a peevish rustle the breeze eddied a handful of leaves around in a circle. Lindsay took it as a warning, remembering that when Renae sassed back, she was inclined to do so with a vengeance. Focusing on the page again, she gave it a more careful perusal.

The featured item in the sale advertisement was a bookcase. A three-shelf oak bookcase quite similar in appearance to the one in her own room.

The room that had been Renae's.

With a little gasp, Lindsay sagged back against the base of the gazebo. Why hadn't she thought about books? Her diligent search had led her to Renae's clothing, but she realized now that she'd been looking in the wrong places to turn up old reading material. There must have been quite a lot of it at one time. Helga Jensen, who lived next door and whose bedroom looked across at Renae's, had told Erik of how the other girl had sat up late, night after night, reading to pass the time after Nils's departure.

The last vestiges of twilight were almost gone, and small, familiar night noises had started up. It was not only the sounds around her that had changed, Lindsay decided. The persistent air of desolation she'd noticed hovering around the derelict structure seemed to have eased.

It was almost as if the grief that had lingered here had been tempered by hope.

"Thank you," Lindsay whispered into the shadows. "I promise you we'll do our best, Erik and I, to learn the truth and share it with you." She took a step toward the house, then glanced back again at the decaying summerhouse. "Oh, and, Renae?

I'm sorry for sounding as if I doubted Nils. In my heart I knew he would never have stayed away on purpose."

Three hours later Lindsay threw up her hands in defeat. She was powdered with dust from having sorted through every carton of books in the attic — and not an inch closer to tracing Nils Thorvaldsen than when she set out to visit the gazebo.

All her mother's ancestors seemed to have been voracious readers. A variety of magazines from as far back as the Gay Nineties had been saved and neatly boxed. As for books, every family member had his or her favorites. Lindsay came across Renae's name scrawled on the flyleaves of novels by Willa Cather, F. Scott Fitzgerald, and Gene Stratton Porter, along with many other popular authors of the era. She also found not one but two dog-eared copies of *Ramona* by Helen Hunt Jackson. Even without opening the tearstained covers she knew who had owned them. As a teenager she herself had read that old-fashioned tearjerker that told of the star-crossed romance between a boy and a girl from opposing cultures.

The tragic love story must have rung a mournful bell for Renae. But if she had kept love letters from Nils between the pages, they were no longer there. Lindsay carefully riffled through every book without finding so much as a postcard.

Wearily she got up at last and started down the attic steps. She was filthy from the search, sore from her bout with the wind, heartsick from failure.

If the past is the key to the future, she thought disconsolately, *there can't be much togetherness in store for Erik and me.*

As if the thought of the big, blond Viking had the power to summon him in person, Lindsay heard the clamor of the metal knocker thundering against the door downstairs.

"Erik! It must be almost midnight!"

"Tell me about it." The young man cooling his heels on the front step had grease smudges on his face and hands and a three-cornered tear in the rolled-up sleeve of the blue shirt that just that afternoon had looked brand-new. He was all but reeling from fatigue, but sparks of exasperation blazed in his eyes as he strode inside.

"Lindsay Dorsett, didn't I warn you that I'd be back tonight if I had to lasso a cow to get here?" His rough tone couldn't quite conceal his relief at finding her safe and sound. "Where the devil have you been?

There've been lights blazing ever since I showed up an hour ago, but no answer at either door. Same with the phone. I jogged all the way down to the gas station to use their outside booth, without any results. If you hadn't answered this time, I'd have tried the police station next to see if you'd been hauled in for speeding."

All he'd gone through to get hold of her that evening gave her an insight into his state of mind. Erik cared about her, Lindsay realized. Nothing reinforced this conviction so much as the quick glimpse she'd caught of the massive John Deere tractor parked at the curb before the door banged behind him and he started letting off steam. Apparently, whatever had gone wrong with his truck had proved to be unfixable at short notice. But to Erik, a promise was a promise. He had called from his uncle's farm to say she could count on him coming back . . . and here he was.

"To help with the bail?" she picked up on his last comment. "That was thoughtful of you, Erik, but you know I haven't been driving so fast since I traded in the 'Vette. It never occurred to me you'd be worried about me. I've been here on the property the whole time."

Hands on hips, he took in her bedraggled appearance. "Doing what? I figured you might be celebrating the grand opening Gladrags had. But to tell the truth, Lin, you look like you've been out cleaning the fishpond."

Lindsay slumped wearily down on the carpeted stairs. It seemed like weeks had passed since she'd ushered him and Uncle Olin out that door. But it was only a few hours.

Eventful, exhausting hours.

"Nothing so useful," she murmured. "I went down to the gazebo."

Erik sank down beside her on the third step from the bottom. He gathered up one of her small, grubby hands between both his grimy paws and looked past the fatigue dulling her dark, luminous da Silva eyes.

"If we live to be a hundred, I doubt you'll ever quit surprising me, Lin. Why did you go to the gazebo? I didn't think you believed —"

"In what you'd told me about Renae still being there after all these years?" Lindsay gazed so intently into Erik's eyes that she could almost see the shimmers of his soul behind the blue irises. "I knew *you* believed, and I had felt something . . . strange . . . down there myself. But in my life there never seemed to be time to spend looking backward. Then the other night —"

Erik knew full well which night it was she referred to. The night he had botched the job of asking her to marry him. He wished he could do an instant replay of that particular five or ten minutes. If he had it to do again, he'd only tell her what was in his heart. The joy he felt when he looked at her or heard her voice. The pride he felt in the way she had reorganized her life, embracing her heritage with wide-flung arms and using it as a tool to a better future.

"I was wrong to insist on dredging up the past," he apologized.

Lindsay wondered whether Nils and Renae had ever sat in this very spot. Talking things over, making plans. Plans for all those tomorrows that had never arrived.

She shook her head. "What you said made me face up to the necessity for building our future on a solid foundation instead of on a past riddled with questions and pitfalls. I vowed that as soon as I got the grand opening out of the way, I would buckle down and spend as long as it took to do what you asked me to do at the very beginning. But then tonight I realized I couldn't put it off any longer. I — I decided to try a shortcut."

Erik didn't understand. "A shortcut to finding the letters?"

Lindsay bobbed her head, pushing back her tangled hair as it flopped into her eyes and then quickly slipping her hand back into Erik's warm, dependable hold.

"Yes. This is a huge house, Erik. It could take months and months and months to search it properly, and — and I don't want problems keeping us apart even one day longer if we can avoid them. The sensible course seemed to be to go ask Renae what she did with the letters."

Erik tucked her head onto his shoulder and gave way to helpless laughter. "Sweetheart, I'm sure glad there's nobody here but us, or they'd haul us both off to. . . . Sensible? To go talk to a ghost?"

Lindsay sat up and looked him straight in the eye. "You believe in her, Erik. Don't try to tell me you don't."

"No, I could never deny it," he agreed. "So, after talking with me on the phone you went down to ask Renae what she did with the letters. Did she tell you?"

"She tried. She really did." Lindsay drew a shuddery breath as she remembered herself trapped in a whirlwind, helpless as a tumbleweed. "Once she calmed down, she handed me a great clue. Except. . . ."

"Except?"

She looked down in distress at their intertwined hands. "Except that she was wrong, Erik. I've been searching for hours. There weren't any letters with her books. Not one!"

Chapter Nine

Erik hadn't felt this shook-up since he was five years old and had caught his first glimpse of Renae. "What do you mean, 'once she calmed down'?" he zeroed in on the crux of Lindsay's narration. "Start at the beginning and tell me exactly what happened."

Uncomfortably, she relived for his benefit the eerie sensations she'd felt as she stepped onto the gazebo's platform. It was almost as if she could hear again the deep, breathless silence in which the dilapidated old structure was steeped and feel once more the presence of a watcher her eyes had not been able to detect.

"An atmosphere like that would have made a believer out of the staunchest skeptic," she declared. "Erik, I *knew* Renae was listening to every word I said. When she refused to answer, I — I got mad and yelled at her. In fact, I stuck my foot right into my mouth."

Erik groaned when he heard that she had actually dared to question Nils's faithfulness aloud. Her description of Renae's impassioned, frightening rebuttal had him shaking his head in awe.

"Any presence that can summon a raging whirlwind on a calm June night is a force to be reckoned with." He brushed an apple leaf out of her hair, smoothing the black tangles back from her brow. "Promise me you won't go down there anymore."

"No, I can't do that," Lindsay denied his request. "I told her that we were going to try to trace Nils through his letters, and I gave her my word that we would let her know what we found out. She's counting on us, Erik." A sigh shook her dusty frame. "Unfortunately, the pointer she tried to give me turned out to be useless. I don't suppose any of us will ever learn the answer to our questions."

"Hold it a minute," Erik said with a frown. "That's the second time you've mentioned a clue Renae gave you. Did you actually hear her say something?"

Lindsay shook her head and stood up. Carefully she fished the folded old sheet of newsprint from her jeans pocket. Smoothing it out and handing it to Erik, she explained how it had come sailing through the air toward her down at the gazebo.

"Upstairs in Renae's old room there's a bookcase which closely resembles that one," she commented. "But all the books must have been hauled up to the attic years ago. That's what I was doing tonight, the reason I couldn't hear the phone or the door knocker. I was up there hunting through box after box of books. But that's *all* I found. Just books."

He was staring at the tattered page as though mesmerized. "Did you search the bookcase?"

Poor guy must be as tired as she was, Lindsay thought. "Erik, I told you: The bookcase was empty," she said patiently. "When I moved in, there wasn't so much as a pamphlet on the shelves."

"That's not what I meant." A wide, excited grin lit up his face. "Remember I told you that Nils was a woodworker? Not an ordinary one, either. A real wizard who loved his work. He made several pieces of furniture for his mother that are treasured family heirlooms to this very day. When Knud and Shelby got married, Uncle Olin passed on to them an oak breakfront that Nils made when he was sixteen. A panel springs open disclosing a secret cubbyhole if you touch your fingernail to a hidden catch in a special way."

Excitement began to evaporate Lindsay's fatigue. "Do you think that Nils might have made that bookcase for Renae?"

"What better present could he give the girl he adored than something he had fashioned with his own two hands? The idea of building a concealed compartment into an ordinary-looking bookcase must have had a special appeal in this case. He was well aware that the da Silvas thought he wasn't good enough for their daughter."

"Come on — let's go find out!"

Bolting up the stairs, Lindsay made for the room she'd been occupying. She scooped several volumes on antiques and vintage clothing off the shelves to give Erik clear access to all the bookcase's surfaces.

It took him several painstaking minutes to find the inconspicuous catch. Suddenly, then, the second time he traced his fingers across the oak uprights, what had appeared to be one board separated into halves, springing open with a protesting creak. Peering in, they saw a hollow crevice spacious enough to contain several packets of letters. The dry rustle of paper met Erik's probing fingers when he reached inside to empty the cache of its contents.

Without thinking twice, Lindsay dumped her best dress shoes out of their box and held the cardboard container while Erik stacked the letters in it.

"Bring them downstairs and I'll make us some cocoa to sip while we look at them," she suggested. "Are they all from Nils?"

"Yes, every one." Erik arranged the letters in the box according to their postmarks, earliest on top, as they hurried back downstairs. "This seems to be the first," he said, following Lindsay into the kitchen. "It's stamped Campbelltown, Michigan, and dated October 5, 1924." He dropped into a chair, scanning the closely written paragraphs. "That's a little place about forty miles north of Grand Rapids, apparently. He paints a word picture of it for Renae, telling her about the beautiful fall colors, which were at the height of their glory right about then."

Lindsay stirred Nestlé Quik into a pan of milk and set it on the stove. "I imagine Michigan's climate was lots different from California's mild weather," she remarked thoughtfully. "I hope he had something warm to wear."

Erik was scanning the next page. "Well, if he hadn't brought a coat along, he would have soon been able to afford some heavy winter clothes. He tells Renae that Joshua Breckinridge, the master furniture crafts-

man he'd come East to study with, had im mediately signed him to a six month apprenticeship. He'd been assigned livir quarters over the workshop and invited t take his meals with the family. It sounds a if it was a case of 'like at first sight' be tween Nils and Mr. and Mrs. Breckinridg and their eight-year-old daughter, Polly."

Although Erik and Lindsay made a con scientious effort to skip the more persona sections of the letters where Nils poured out his unwavering love for Renae, it was clear that he was counting the days until he could return for her so they could be mar ried. Muffling yawns until they could be concealed no longer, they made their way through the rest of the correspondence dated 1924, then admitted that they needed sleep before proceeding further.

Erik pushed away the cup containing the dregs of his cocoa. He stood up, scrubbing a hand across his eyes.

"I'll bunk down at Gunnar's house nex door," he said, adding that he was in n shape to travel any farther that night. "Un cle Olin's tractor will be all right out ther in the street for a few hours. I'll get it bac to him first thing in the morning. Arne ar Ingrid offered to pick up the spare part need to fix the truck. They'll run them

to the farm on their way home from church. With luck, I can be back here soon after lunch tomorrow."

Lindsay picked up the shoe box from the table and held it out to him. "Want to take this along?"

"Nope. We'll look at the rest of them together," Erik insisted. "That way, we'll both know at the same time whether or not Nils jilted Renae."

"I already know." Lindsay remembered that this point had been the central controversy of the long-standing feud between their families. She set the box down again and held out her hand in contrite apology. "On behalf of all the da Silvas, I'd like to apologize to the Thorvaldsens for suspecting Nils of being untrue to Renae. She nearly tore my head off tonight for suggesting such a thing."

"What better evidence could we ask?" Turning the handshake into a hug, Erik brought her with him to the door and kissed her tenderly. "All these years I've been convinced that Nils and Renae had a love to last for all time. After falling in love with you, I was almost envious of him. I wanted the same thing to happen to me."

"It has, Erik." How foolish of her to have thought that grand passions were only for

the very young, Lindsay thought. "All my life, for as long as I draw breath, and for the rest of eternity as well, I'm going to love a man named Erik Thorvaldsen."

The following afternoon Lindsay and Erik sat down eagerly together to read the rest of the letters. The final one in the stack was postmarked March 27, 1925. In it, Nils declared that within hours he would be on his way home to California. He wanted to be with the girl he loved on her birthday.

Thoroughly perplexed, Lindsay looked up from the firm masculine handwriting that covered several sheets of lined paper. "I don't understand," she murmured. "Nils has the train schedule down pat. He assures Renae that he'll be arriving on the afternoon of March thirty-first."

"Her twenty-first birthday," Erik put in. "She'd be free to do as she wished that day. Nils still had six more months to wait before he came of age, but even if his parents had continued to refuse their permission for their son's marriage, it wouldn't have kept the couple apart any longer. Mr. Breckinridge was ready to make Nils a junior partner in the furniture company. He and his wife enclosed a little note with this letter, inviting Renae to be their houseguest for the next six months if the wedding had to be postponed that long."

"What could have gone wrong?"

"I don't know, but we're going to find out. We owe Renae the answer — as well as ourselves." Erik pushed his chair back from the table and held out his hand to Lindsay. "Let's go put that antique phone of yours to work. It's hopeless to think that Joshua Breckinridge might still be alive after all these years, but we might get real lucky and find his daughter, Polly."

Lindsay headed toward the parlor at his side. "At least we have a starting place now."

The operators at Directory Assistance did their best. Nevertheless, none of them succeeded in tracing a party named Polly Breckinridge in any of the small Michigan towns in the vicinity of Nils Thorvaldsen's last-known address.

"She probably got married and changed her name half a century ago," Erik grumbled.

Lindsay made a suggestion. "See if Campbelltown has a local newspaper."

It did not. However, persistent inquiries turned up a listing for a small weekly published in nearby Whitewater Falls. The *Ga-*

zette's office wasn't open on Sundays. Next morning, Erik made an early stop at Lindsay's house on the way to work. Thanks to the three-hour time difference between Michigan and California, a connection was easily established.

After explaining his quest, Erik was transferred to the research librarian in charge of the newspaper's "morgue." Copies of the *Gazette* dating back to 1908 were available on microfilm, she proudly assured him. She had no luck locating any mention of a person named Nils Thorvaldsen at the specific time he inquired about. Where Joshua Breckinridge was concerned, it was a different story.

Erik filled a whole page with notes. Then he thanked the woman for all her help and hung up with a gesture of finality.

Lindsay was learning to read his expression very well. "It's bad news, isn't it?" she guessed.

"Catastrophic." He paused for a moment as if reluctant to go on, then went ahead and got it over with. "The day after Nils wrote that letter planning to join Renae on her birthday, Joshua Breckinridge, his wife Flora, and three employees of their company were all killed when a tornado ripped through their property."

"How horrible! What about the little girl?"

"No — fortunately she was at a friend's house when the twister hit. The woman I just talked to found some information about her in an April issue of the *Gazette*. It said that after being orphaned, Polly had gone to live with an aunt and uncle in Detroit." His broad shoulders slumped in discouragement. "Detroit! Lindsay, that's a *huge* city! For a while there, it seemed like we were getting close. But I doubt we'll *ever* learn what happened to Nils now."

"Oh! You mean he wasn't —"

"In that workshop with the others when the roof caved in on them?" Erik shook his head. "All three employees were older men, natives of the locality. Their names were listed in the paper. Nils must have already been on his way to catch the train when the storm struck. But the nearest railhead was considerably south of Campbelltown. Nobody — with the possible exception of Polly Breckinridge, if she's still alive — knows exactly when he left or what route he took."

As far as the two of them were concerned, the newly discovered letters were proof positive that Nils had never had any intention of jilting Renae. But fate had stepped in in some unknown way and prevented him from returning to her.

"Do you think that if you told Uncle Olin what we've learned, it would make him feel better about quarreling with his brother and inheriting the farm in his place?" Lindsay asked.

Erik gave his head a discouraged shake. "He's contended all along that Nils never did anything dishonorable. And the feud would have been over even if we hadn't found the letters. But without some solid evidence as to what caused his brother to stay away forever, he'll never stop blaming himself for his part in that old tragedy."

The return address on Nils's letters had helped trace him up to a point, just as they'd hoped. But now they'd run into a real dead end.

"It's the same with Renae," Lindsay admitted. "She died not knowing what had happened to Nils. She's still waiting. If we never find out —"

"Then she's no worse off than she was before," Erik said. A glance at his watch made him push aside the notepad he'd been using and take a hasty step toward the front door. Then he turned back and took her in his arms for a mournful hug. "It's you and me I'm worried about, Lin.

Nils and Renae — they're gone. We have our whole lives ahead of us. Don't we?"

Each dawn brought the birth of Shelby's twins twenty-four hours closer. Day by day the wedding between Marta and Tony approached. July was next on the calendar, and with it the exciting Scandinavian trip Karin and Dannel were planning to visit the homelands of both their ancestors.

For Erik and Lindsay, however, the future seemed to have been placed permanently on hold. They were in love, yet he hadn't repeated his proposal. She hadn't said anything about making a commitment.

How could they? The past had them by the throat.

Nearly two weeks dragged by, with Gladrags doing fairly well and the short façade restoration Erik had been commissioned to do before starting the major job for Clayton and Eva Simms nearly complete.

Lindsay woke early that morning and lay still, with no motivation to move, staring at the misty reflection of the gazebo floating in Renae's Art Deco mirror. Even with the sunlight limning it, the weatherbeaten old structure seemed grayer than it had a week earlier. As if desolation had started closing in on it again.

The same sort of miasma could warp their whole lives.

"Not if we don't let it," Lindsay murmured, sitting up in bed and starting to think hard about the alternatives. She tossed back the blankets and headed for the door without stopping to hunt for her slippers.

Something had to be done!

Chapter Ten

Afterward the terrible fear that haunted Lindsay's dreams was that history might be repeating itself.

She couldn't make herself forget that it had been Renae, in the autumn of 1924, who had learned of a promising career opportunity for Nils. Renae who had urged her young fiancé to leave her temporarily behind in California while he journeyed to Michigan to serve his apprenticeship. Now, nearly seventy years later, it was she, Renae's great-niece, who had unearthed a slender clue to Polly Breckinridge's present whereabouts. The man she loved — another Thorvaldsen — insisted on flying East to investigate that lead.

And she was responsible.

"I'm flabbergasted. This is fantastic!" Stopping by after work the day Lindsay made up her mind to take action, Erik was overjoyed at all the information she had managed to garner by long-distance telephone. "Where did you dig out these facts? The *Gazette* never reported the names of the aunt and uncle who took Polly in after her parents were killed."

"I know." Lindsay said she had figured there was about a one out of four chance of them also being called Breckinridge.

"They were, by the way," she added. "But I didn't find out until later that it was Joshua's older brother and his wife and children who made a place in their home for Polly. When I started dialing this morning, the only certain thing I had to go on was that an eight-year-old child would have to go to school no matter where she lived. So first I got through to Patrick Henry Elementary in Campbelltown. Then I coaxed them into checking to see where that little girl's academic records had been transferred to in the spring of 1925."

Erik scanned the pages of notes recorded in her neat handwriting. "You did more than that. Imagine parlaying a few third-grade marks for spelling and arithmetic into a Detroit street address, phone number, and the name of her guardians!"

Lindsay was thrilled to hear the excitement in his voice and to notice the way his tense shoulders had relaxed. What a terrible burden he had been carrying around all these years!

It seemed cruel to throw cold water on

that cheerful enthusiasm of his. Still, it would be worse to let him go on believing that she had pulled a miracle out of the hat.

"I was awfully lucky to learn as much as I did," she conceded. "Unfortunately, I lost track of the family in April of 1932."

Neither Polly nor her cousins had finished out that school year, so far as Lindsay had been able to ascertain. The Breckinridges had just suddenly packed up and moved away.

"Probably because they could no longer pay the rent," she guessed, sighing. "I read somewhere that during the worst years of the Great Depression, more than half the wage earners in big cities were thrown out of work. Polly's uncle must have lost his job. Maybe he found employment in some other town. Or maybe the whole family just turned into gypsies, picking up seasonal work whenever they could to keep body and soul together. With so many people on the move, it was impossible to find out."

Erik slid his arm around Lindsay's shoulder and gave her an affectionate squeeze. "I'm amazed that you had the persistence to keep on checking public records after hitting a roadblock like that. In fact, it's absolutely incredible that you managed to pick up this information about her marriage in 1939."

That was what had been worrying Lindsay. That it was too incredible to be true.

"*Maybe* I picked up the record of her marriage." Uncertainty came through in the way she stressed the word. "I had no way of making sure it was really our Polly Breckinridge who married Eugene Harvey that year. It's not that uncommon a name, you know. It could be someone entirely different whose marriage was listed as a vital statistic in the records I checked."

"Okay. I'll try not to get too optimistic. But whoever participated in that wedding, it took place more than half a century ago," Erik mentioned in a practical tone. "Do you know if this Mrs. Eugene Harvey is still alive?"

"Yes. That was fairly easy because she was a member of a union. Once I found that out, I could trace her right up to the present without any trouble because their insurance is still paying her bills."

Lindsay said that the woman, who had to be well into her seventies by now, had been widowed a few years back. Quite recently she'd been experiencing some health problems of her own. "A few months ago she entered a convalescent hospital in Kalamazoo. The supervisor there informed me that Mrs. Harvey is very hard of hearing. She never uses the phone."

"That complicates matters."

"Shall we try writing her a letter?" Lindsay suggested tentatively. "She could dictate a reply to a nurse if she's not up to answering it herself. What we mainly need to know at first is if she really is the Polly Breckinridge whose parents were killed in that tornado."

"It would be much better if I flew out there and talked to her in person. If she is who we hope she is, she may be able to tell me right then and there what my great-uncle's plans were. Elderly people often have near total recall about events that happened in their youth."

Lindsay was looking unhappy at the thought of his making the trip, Erik realized. As tactfully as possible, he reminded her that a woman of Mrs. Harvey's age might not be around indefinitely for them to question at their leisure. "Besides, I just finished up my current project. That gives me a week's breathing space before I have to start on the major remodel in Old Town Eureka."

The coincidences between the trip Erik was contemplating and the one Nils had embarked on had every alarm bell in Lindsay's system screaming. It wasn't the distance. With modern air schedules he could go and return in a matter of hours. But Nils had had that train schedule all figured out too.

"Oh, Erik, I don't know. . . ."

Taking her by the shoulders, he turned her to face him. "Look, Lindsay, my great-uncle's mysterious disappearance cost at least one life and ruined several others. I don't intend to let it ruin ours."

More than once he'd told her where he stood on that subject. "In other words, we have to resolve the past before we have any business talking about the future?"

"Before we *dare* talk about the future would be more like it." Erik drew her closer, taking courage from the strong, steady rhythm of her heart beating against his chest. Lindsay was made for him; he'd known it since the first moment he set eyes on her. It absolutely terrified him to think that something unforeseen might prevent them from spending the rest of their lives together.

"This will be a new experience for me," he said, thrusting the harrowing fear aside.

"Do you know, I've never been on an airplane in my whole life?"

Now and then Lindsay had the odd conviction that she had known Erik far longer than just a few months. An occasional inflection in his voice or the yearning way he touched her hair gave a deep, penetrating glimpse into his inner thoughts and feelings. He needed all the confidence she could instill in him, she suddenly realized. Encouragement, not any more fearful reminders of how much he and Nils Thorvaldsen already had in common.

"Oh, there's nothing to flying," she assured him with false blitheness. "Just remember to keep your seat belt fastened."

They were going to make a great pair, Erik thought, feeling a renewal of courage seep through his veins. As a matter of fact, this trip was probably just what he'd been needing. It could serve as a practice run for the honeymoon flight to Hawaii or Jamaica or wherever that he soon hoped to take with this beguiling woman. If he was very lucky, she would never need to know that venturing any higher into the air than the top rung of his ladder had always scared the living daylights out of him.

Three days later Lindsay dropped the

cloche hat she'd been adjusting on a stand and made a dive for the telephone. Her breathless "Hello!" brought a rueful chuckle from the man on the other end.

"Sorry for not touching base with you earlier," Erik apologized. "I just got back to my hotel room. There wasn't a chance to speak privately before this."

He had called her that morning from O'Hare, where he was waiting to change planes for the short hop from Chicago to Kalamazoo. Lindsay hadn't drawn a panic-free breath since.

"Any luck in getting an appointment with Mrs. Harvey?" she asked, trying to sound very calm and matter-of-fact.

"The nurse kept me cooling my heels for about three hours until the doctor showed up to make his regular rounds and gave permission. It wasn't a boring wait, though, not by any means," Erik said. "I spent most of the time flirting with a de-lightful old lady in a wheelchair. Her name is Wilhelmina Wallace. We sat in the rest home's TV room watching game shows to-gether. If I ever get on *Jeopardy!*, I just hope she isn't one of my opponents."

Lindsay had a hunch he was rambling on to give her a chance to catch her breath. It was no good trying to put on an act with him. Even over long distance he seemed able to tune in to her private thoughts and fears.

"What about Mrs. Harvey, Erik?" she interrupted. "*Is* she our Polly Breckinridge?"

"The one and only," he said jubilantly. Polly had remembered exactly who Nils was, he said, not adding that for a few confusing minutes she had mistaken him for his great-uncle. "Turns out that at the age of eight she'd had an enormous crush on him. She'd even convinced her father to let her ride along in his Model T that last day when he drove Nils to the bus station."

"*Bus* station!"

Erik explained that the nearest railhead was a considerable distance from the small community where the Breckinridge family lived. "The bus left Campbelltown in plenty of time to connect with the westbound train. Unfortunately, it never arrived at the station." In a somber tone, Erik confided that he had finally learned why his great-uncle had never returned home. "Polly's information about watching Nils board that bus dovetailed so closely with Mrs. Wallace's account of the violent series of tornados that killed hundreds of people in the Midwest on the same day, I decided to check it out at the library."

Sure enough, he reported, the local newspapers of the time carried graphic accounts by eyewitnesses who had watched in horror while a twister toppled a busload of travelers off a bridge, into the storm-whipped waters of the river far below.

"There weren't any survivors." Erik dragged in an emotional breath. "In fact, most of the bodies were washed away on the current, clear out to Lake Michigan."

"Oh, Erik, those *poor people!* And think of the families who never knew what had happened to their loved ones!"

"What made Nils's disappearance so complete was the fact that Mr. and Mrs. Breckinridge both died in another tornado that same day. No one was left to put two and two together when their prize apprentice failed to return. And because of the tornado's destructiveness, none of Nils's belongings were left to search even if an acquaintance had suspected the truth."

A sudden thought struck Lindsay. "When did this happen, Erik? The exact date?"

"On March 28, 1925. In that single day more than eight hundred people were killed in tornados that cut a swath of destruction up and down the heartland of the country."

"And Renae died exactly one year later. What a sad, strange coincidence!"

Privately, Erik thought that if Nils and Renae had been as much in tune as he and Lindsay were, it wasn't such a strange coincidence at all. Renae must have known that something terrible had happened to Nils. She just didn't know what and where and how.

"Speaking of Renae," he said, "when I duplicated the newspaper accounts of the bus disaster for Uncle Olin, I made an extra copy of everything. I thought perhaps we could take them down. . . ."

"To the gazebo? Oh, Erik, thank you! That was exactly the right thing to do," Lindsay praised his foresight. "I've felt terrible being unable to keep my end of the bargain after her clue led us to those letters. Were you able to record Polly's story on the tape cassette as you planned?"

"Yes, and it won't be any bother to have that duplicated too. It will give me something to do in Chicago during that ninety-minute layover tomorrow while I'm waiting for my flight out to San Francisco." He paused. "Listen, Lindsay, there's really no need for you to drive all the way down to the city to meet me. I can easily hop a bus home, over the Golden Gate Bridge —"

"Not on your life!" Lindsay pushed away the nightmare vision this suggestion provoked. Tornados were a rarity in California, but she had no intention of allowing Erik to tempt fate. "Just try to keep me away!"

The wait at SFO turned out to be something of a nightmare in itself. A speedy driver by habit, Lindsay had been lucky to avoid a ticket as she zipped down 101, over the bridge, and through the city, south. Then the wait began. First, rain squalls peppering the Windy City delayed the take-off of Erik's flight. Then, when it was too late to divert it to an alternate destination, fog closed in on SFO as it often did in the summer. Visibility hit zero, and arriving planes were locked into the tight, nervous grid of a holding pattern.

For more than two hours Lindsay sat frozen in her black plastic seat at the arrival gate with her eyes riveted to the electronic board. Praying — hard — for everyone trapped up there above the murky gray mist overhanging the city. Especially for one young man who she suspected might be rather nervous about heights.

Eventually, as it always did, the fog

229

lifted. One by one, the planes came in. And there was Erik, looking more wonderful than she could have dreamed. She welcomed him home with her arms flung wide.

At the height of the summer, the last traces of dusk lingered almost until ten before beaming themselves out across the wide Pacific in search of other lands to light. Even so, and even considering Lindsay's penchant for disregarding the speed limit, it was almost dark by the time she pulled onto the newly resurfaced driveway alongside her wonderful old Butterfat mansion.

She cut the engine with a sigh of relief.

Erik's sigh was louder and even more relieved. "Thanks for the ride, sweetheart," he said. "But if you don't learn to lighten up the pressure with that lead foot of yours, I intend to have a chat with a couple of old pals in the Highway Patrol. Tip them off about an easy way to fill up their ticket quota for the month."

Lindsay gaped at him in horror. "You wouldn't!"

"Oh, yes, I would!"

He popped loose his shoulder harness and swiveled around to look her squarely in the eye. "I love you, Lindsay da Silva Dorsett. I want to marry you and live with you in joy and tranquillity the rest of my life. But I wouldn't have much peace of mind if I had to picture you zooming off to antique sales at ninety miles an hour. Why, the awful worry would likely give me dizzy spells! That would be a terrible thing to do to a man who spends his working day up on a ladder."

Lindsay gulped. He was teasing, of course, about the dizzy spells. Or was he? Even if it meant slowing down to bicycle pace, she'd never deliberately do anything to endanger him.

"I'll reform," she promised. "Starting to-morrow. About the other — You really do love me, Erik? *Me?* Not just because I look so much like —"

"Like Renae?" His tone was utterly as-tonished. "Lin, where did you ever get a wild idea like that?" He caught up one of her hands, those good, capable hands of a modern woman who could manage so many things, and kissed each finger indi-vidually before pressing it to his heart. "To be honest, I never had much respect for Renae until you made me think about how different women were in the twenties. I guess those frivolous clothes the flappers wore should have tipped me off. I just thought of her as vain and silly and lazy — and a terrible coward to let her family dictate to her the way they did. And on top of all that, to sit around the gazebo, weeping, until she caught pneumonia instead of marching back East and moving heaven and earth to find out what had happened to the man she loved. That's what you would have done, isn't it?"

"If you had suddenly disappeared?" Lindsay shivered and reached up to smooth his rumpled blond hair. "Erik, I love you so much it would have cracked my heart right in two. But yes, I'd have taped it together long enough to — to find out for sure. Poor Renae. It wasn't her fault that she wasn't brought up to be a take-charge individual. Girls in those days were expected to be credits to their parents, and sweet companions to their husbands, and loving mothers to their children."

"You'll be all that. And more." In the gloaming, Erik's face was very serious. "Will you marry me, Lindsay? Be my sweet companion for life? Join those salt-water da Silva bloodlines of yours to my landlubber Thorvaldsen strain, and let the world know that the feud is over forever?"

"Yes, thank you," she whispered. "My bloodlines and I will be delighted."

Arms entwined, they made their way into the house. Through the French doors they could catch glimpses of a domed, weatherbeaten structure at the rear of the property.

"It's not completely dark yet. Why don't we take those things down to the gazebo right away?" Lindsay suggested. "Now that we've finally learned the answers to questions that have tormented Renae for nearly seventy years, it seems cruel to make her wait even one extra day."

Erik dug the battery-operated tape recorder and a sheaf of papers from his luggage. Trudging through the orchard, he felt a different atmosphere surrounding the old summerhouse than he'd ever noticed before. The air positively hummed with energy, while expectation had replaced despair.

Once again he thought with admiration of Lindsay's courage in stalking down here all alone the night of Gladrags's grand opening. "Go ahead, honey," he told his future wife. "This is your show."

Lindsay tried to conceal the uneasiness she felt. A few weeks earlier she had been subjected to an awesome demonstration of power from a source she could neither see nor hear. Who knew what would happen this time?

Squaring her shoulders, she slowly mounted the steps of the sagging old summerhouse. "I promised to come back, and I have," she said, feeling a little like Custer holding out a peace pipe to Sitting Bull. "I've brought Erik along. He's the one who went back East and got the answers that are so important to all of us. First, though, we'd like to share some wonderful news with you. We're going to be married. At last, the da Silvas and Thorvaldsens will be united into one family. The feud that started when you and Nils fell in love is over for good."

Distant bells — wedding bells? — seemed to tinkle in the branches of the apple trees. Then the dust alongside the creekbed swirled around in impatient circles.

Taking the hint, Lindsay and Erik worked together to arrange copies of all the news articles along the weathered benches. Then they straightened up and stood together in the center of the platform, keenly aware that they were not really alone.

It was hard to know where to start.

Lindsay did her best. "Remember Joshua Breckinridge's little girl, Polly? Erik went and had a talk with her yesterday. She told him about how she and her father drove Nils to the bus station the day he started home to California to be with you. It's all here on tape. . . ."

"Nothing less powerful than a tornado could have kept him away, Renae." Erik took up the tale when Lindsay looked imploringly at him. "I'm going to make sure my family — Olin and all the others — know that Nils loved you every minute of his life."

There was nothing more to say. In fact, Lindsay now had the distinct impression that their presence was superfluous. Hand in hand with Erik, she walked down the steps for the last time. As they started toward the house she heard a click, as though an invisible hand had turned on the tape recorder.

They were steps away from the back door when a rumbling tremor caused the ground underfoot to buckle and sway. The short, sharp jolt had them scurrying for the doorway in a hurry.

"Ohmigosh!" Lindsay squeaked as they cowered together in the shelter of the protective beams of the old mansion. "You get quakes up here too?"

" 'Fraid so," Erik answered, not quite as nonchalantly as he would have liked. Though earthquakes were a commonplace occurrence in California because of the many fault lines running deep underground, no one really ever gets to the point where he can take them for granted.

Already the rhythmically swaying light fixture above the kitchen table was arcing less wildly, however, and the rumble that for a moment had sounded like a runaway freight train had dwindled, then ceased.

"That would have registered about a four on the Richter scale," Erik guessed knowledgeably. "You don't have to worry about the house, honey. Ferndale's Butterfat mansions withstood a much worse shaking than that in the 1906 quake."

But it wasn't the house Lindsay was concerned with. A new noise that seemed louder yet smaller in scope than the earthquake that had preceded it was coming from the rear of the property.

"Something's happening back there!" she cried. "Come on! I'm afraid that —"

She broke off with a gasp of shock. Pelting through the trees at breakneck speed, they broke into the open just in time to see the last pilings that anchored the gazebo to earth tilt forward, then collapse into Francis Creek.

Phosphorescence silvered the water, illuminating the fast-moving current from below as the debris dipped onto the waves with a mighty splash, then righted itself like a tall, round, domed raft. It headed downstream as if an eagle-eyed Portuguese ship captain had set the course and had a firm hand on the helm.

Lindsay watched until it was nearly out of sight. Then, her face still tinged with awe, she looked up at Erik. "Do you suppose that Renae found a way for them to be together at last?"

"I'd never rule it out," he marveled. "She said she'd love Nils forever, and she didn't budge from this spot until she found out what happened to him." The da Silva women were something else, he conceded. Apparently all Renae had needed to know was that Nils's bus had landed in the water. She'd found a way to bring that old gazebo out to meet him. It wouldn't surprise him in the least to hear of it heading through the Panama Canal a few weeks down the line.

He wrapped his arm around Lindsay. "Let's go home, sweetheart."

The employees of Thorndike Press hope you have enjoyed this Large Print book. All our Large Print titles are designed for easy reading, and all our books are made to last. Other Thorndike Press Large Print books are available at your library, through selected bookstores, or directly from us.

For information about titles, please call:

(800) 257-5157

To share your comments, please write:

Publisher
Thorndike Press
P.O. Box 159
Thorndike, Maine 04986